WATCHTOWER

ANTI-VEHICLE BARRIER / HEDGEHOG

SURFACE BARRIERS / ASPARAGUS GRASS

BORDER SIGNAL FENCE

HINTERLAND FENCE

Going
Over

Going

Over

BETH KEPHART

CHRONICLE BOOKS
SAN FRANCISCO

Library of Congress Cataloging-in-Publication Data:
Kephart, Beth.
 Going Over / Beth Kephart.
    p. cm.
 Summary: In the early 1980s Ada and Stefan are young, would-be lovers living on opposite sides of the Berlin Wall—Ada lives with her mother and grandmother and paints graffiti on the Wall, and Stefan lives with his grandmother in the East and dreams of escaping to the West.
 ISBN 978-1-4521-2457-5 (alk. paper)
 1. Berlin Wall, Berlin, Germany, 1961–1989—Juvenile fiction. 2. Families—Germany—Berlin—Juvenile fiction. 3. Berlin (Germany)—History—1945–1990—Juvenile fiction. [1. Berlin Wall, Berlin, Germany, 1961–1989—Fiction. 2. Family life—Germany—Fiction. 3. Love—Fiction. 4. Berlin (Germany)—History—1945–1989—Fiction. 5. Germany—History—1945–1990—Fiction.] I. Title.
 PZ7.K438We 2014
 813.6—dc23
                                        2012046894

Manufactured in China.

Design by Jennifer Tolo Pierce.
Typeset in Sabon.

10 9 8 7 6 5 4 3 2 1

Chronicle Books LLC
680 Second Street, San Francisco, California 94107

Chronicle Books—we see things differently. Become part of our community at www.chroniclebooks/teen.

for Tamra Tuller, who set the story free

BERLIN

WEST BERLIN

– – – – – – – BERLIN WALL

EAST BERLIN

★ FRIEDRICHSHAIN

★
SO36

HERE

SO36

*

We live with ghosts. We live with thugs, dodgers, punkers, needle ladies, pork knuckle. We live where there's no place else to go. We live with birds—a pair of magpies in the old hospital turrets, a fat yellow-beaked grebe in the thick sticks of the plane trees. A man named Sebastien has moved into the Kiez from France. My mother's got an eye on him.

"You've had enough trouble, Jana," Omi warns her.

Mutti shakes her head, mutters under her breath. Calls her own mother Ilse, like they are sisters, or friends. Like two decades and a war don't divide them. Like sleeping, dreaming, waking, breathing so close has quieted the one to the other.

We live in a forest of box gardens and a city of tile. We live with brick and bullet holes. We live where Marlene Dietrich lived, and the Kaiser and the Reich. We live here, and here is where I have learned what I know, all that I can tell you, including: You can scrub the smell of graffiti out of the air with vanilla, cinnamon, nutmeg, lavender, sometimes oil of roses. But you can never scrub the paint off the wall.

"Be careful, Ada."

Of course I'm careful. I'm in love.

✿

What can I tell you, what should you know? There is a line between us, a wall. It is wide as a river; it has teeth. It is barbed and trenched and tripped and lit and piped and meshed and bricked—155 kilometers of wrong. There are dogs, there are watchtowers, there are men, there are guns, there are blares, but this is West Berlin, the Kreuzberg Kiez, Post Office Sudost 36, and we're free. All of us up and down the Oranienstrasse and the Bethaniendamm, along the Landwehrkanal, beneath the cherry trees, in the run-down Wilhelmines, beside the last stand—all of us here, and the birds, too: We're free.

It's Stefan who I'm worried for. Stefan, on the other side, with his grandmother, Omi's best friend from the war years. In Stefan's Berlin the sky is the factory version of brown, and the air is the stink of boot treads and coal. On the dead-end streets the cars rattle like toys, the Vopos march, the kids wear the same shoes. In the brown velour living rooms with the burgundy rugs, test patterns crunch the TVs.

"Don't exaggerate, Ada," Mutti says.

I'm not. I've seen. I've known Stefan since I was two years old, loved him since the day I turned twelve. That's three long years of loving Stefan in a city that keeps us apart. Two cities.

If you could see him, you would understand. Stefan is sunflower tall with deep blue eyes and thick, curling hair. He's the strongest apprentice at the Eisfabrik on Köpenicker Strasse, which makes the shoulders of his shirts too small. He knows all the words to Depeche Mode songs and his hands are broad, his fingers thin and truthy. Whenever we go, my Omi and me—to the Friedrichstrasse stop, up the long flight of stairs, past the Vopos and the Vopos' eyes, all the way down to Stefan's place— he takes me out onto his balcony and shows me the world through the eye of his telescope. In the cold, in the rain, in the snow, in the sun, we stand in a city of spies—our grandmothers behind us in the living room, knee to knee, remembering the Russians so that someday, maybe, they'll forget them. Below us, the wall is a zigzag stitch and the river runs divided. The Brandenburg Gate hints gold. The trams shake their tracks. St. Thomas is two towers and a dome, a polished spit of spindle. I press my eye against the cool glass piece. Berlin rises and falls and the wall fogs in. Stefan tips the telescope up—angling toward the stars.

"See?" Stefan will say.

"I see," I'll answer.

Because no one can stop us from looking.

It would be easier, Mutti says, to love a boy from my own neighborhood. It would be much more convenient. There are so many rules, when you cross, West to East. Rights that you pay for, and not just with marks: They smile at you weird, sniff through your stuff, X-ray their eyeballs straight through you. "What is your business?" they ask you. My business is love. Lopsided love, because the path is one way. You don't get out from the East unless you're somebody special, or they plain don't want you anymore.

But look at Mutti and how she's lived, the opposite of easy. Look at us in this squatters' town, making it but barely. You could say that we're free in SO36, and you could claim that we're the punkiest zip code. Still, things are missing; things haven't been found.

"I want a dad," I would say when I was a kid. "I want a father; where is he?" I would sit on Mutti's lap, watching her coffee steam. I would pull at her braids with my fingers. She would say, "One day, Ada. One day he'll come." I was ten before I understood that she was lying.

✳

I wait until it's so black night that the dogs are already lazy with their dreams. I wrap a shirt around my aerosols and my flashlight, my skinnies and my fats, and stuff it all into my sack. I fix a bandana on my face, yank up a hood, pull on a pair of gloves, open the door, close it. *Good night, Mutti.* I walk the long line of hall, then the outside stairs down, past all the other doors of all the other people who make it their business to live here—the carpenters and cooks and Jesus freaks, the hashish entrepreneurs, the old ladies, my best girl friend in the universe, whose name is Arabelle. The courtyard is blue with the late-night TVs. The air is eggplant and sausage. Arabelle's parade of a bike is where Arabelle leaves it—beneath the window box of Timur's flat, where he's growing groves of basil.

When the magpies are out, they stripe the night. When the moon is lit, it finds me. My sack on my back, my Adidas on the pedals, I push my way out onto the street and ride the cobblestones beneath the scaffolding and flutter, and the shawls hanging off the railings. I ride past the sleeping caravans and through the green-gray night of the Mariannenplatz—the old turrets of the old hospital casting their shadows and the soft wool streamers of Arabelle's bike kicking up around me. At the far end of the platz, the top of St. Thomas Church gets lost in the clouds, like an ornament wrapped up in cotton. I go as far as I can inside the crack of cold, skim the wide belly of the church, hang on to my breakneck speed. I brake before the wall slams me.

I work alone and in nobody's hurry. I work from my one black book and from the things that I know about sky and vanishing, fear and wanting. I tilt the flashlight up on the bricked-in windowsill behind me and stand inside its shine, the cans of color at my feet and the rabbits on the opposite side of the wall, looking for nibbles in the death zone. There's nothing like heat in this light. There's only what I'm graffing—the swirls and orbs and flecks and tags, the pictures I'm making for Stefan. Precision is the trick of the wrist. Curves jet from the shoulder. If you want a halo bigger than you've earned the right to be, you paint with your whole body. You can use your thumb to spare your index finger, but you can't lose your nerve, or your reason.

I work in fractions. I take my time. I listen for the guards in their tower, the knick-click of the rifles, the scrape inside the binocular barrels, the dogs on long, stinking leashes. I click the flashlight on and off to make my wicks and glyphs dance, and then I pack myself up and ride Arabelle's bike to the viewing platform on the West Berlin side. I leave the bike and climb.

"Hey!" I call from up there. "Hey! Hey!" Leaning as far as I can over the platform railing and waving my arms toward the East—my arms and my broad, arcing yellow light, which paints the night sky brighter. I squint against the crack of cold, daring the Stasi to see me. If Stefan's awake, Stefan will find me with the convex and concave lenses of his grandfather's old scope. If he can see the moon, then he can see me, painting his Welcome Here sign.

"My graffs are good," I tell Stefan, when I see him. "It's art, pure and true." He says I should take a picture and bring it to him, stick it inside my boot so that the border guards can't find it. I say taking a picture would ruin the surprise, and if he can't come see my art for himself someday, then he can't be my boyfriend—not forever. Look at yourself, I tell him. Look and imagine yourself free.

"Anything could happen," Mutti says, to warn me when I get home, at whatever time it is, however long it takes me. Anything. Because the wall does not belong to West Berlin, and neither does the ground where I stand when I'm painting. I am a public enemy, a property defacer. I am an artist in love with a boy.

Anything can happen. But then again, what hasn't happened already? I ride Arabelle's bike home and the birds watch me fly. My paint cans clang together in their pack. I skid to a stop, pull the front gate open, weave through the courtyards shaped like keyholes. I prop Arabelle's parade of a bike back up beneath the basil and climb the clinking outside steps. I walk on my Adidas toes and keep my courier bag of colors quiet until I'm back in the room that we share.

Omi, Mutti, and me. Three in three rooms, sliding away from each other.

FRIEDRICHSHAIN

★

She has pink hair, a big pop of Bazooka color. She cuts it straight across, Cleopatra style, with scissors that she borrows from the co-op. Out in the night she shines like some West Berliner planet.

"Did you see me?" That's her question. "Did you see me up there waving to you?"

You tell her yes. It makes her happy. It isn't a lie, not every time. A splash of color will flash your scope and you'll think that it's her; think she's found you. Three letters and two syllables. That's her name, and it fits her.

She brings you basil leaves in summer and electric pop all year round. She hides chocolate in her pockets. She tears pages out of the books she likes and leaves them on your table. Once she showed up at the door in a spackled leather jacket, worn and beaten, she was boasting, by some surfboard-sanding punker.

"It's yours," she said, and when she took it off, her arms were freckled color. She's a graffiti genius, if you believe what she says. Cocky looks good on Ada.

There's nothing she believes in less than black and white, or gray. Even the mole she paints above her lip is green sometimes, and sometimes orange, and the mole trades sides above her lip depending on the season. She wasn't always like this. She was a little kid once. You remember her even when she won't remember herself. Ponytails and questions. Big eyes. "Why not?" "What's this?" "Can I?" It's right there. In your head. Who she was before she had the power of being anyone at all.

"This is Ada."

"This is Stefan."

She was bored out of her mind. She'd drive you crazy. You'd be out on the balcony and she'd show up and want. Asking for it, always. Why. Why is the air thick blue up high and thin blue at the edges? What is the color of blur? Which one is Mars, and why does Cygnus fly south, and what do you mean: four-power finder scope? Why don't you get a bigger power? The only cure for her was a pencil. Give her one of those and a chart of the skies and at least she'd sit for a minute, looking and tracing, putting a shine on the belt of Orion, a couple of bows on the tail of Centaurus, fire in the mouth of Draco.

"I need paints," she'd say.

"I need pastels."

One day she showed up and she was twelve years old. She'd cut her long hair short, painted a stripe of blond that hung across one eye. She wore a hoop in one ear, nothing in the other. She had that mole on her lip. It could have been purple. Glitter, you think you remember.

"I'm Ada," she said, like you were going to argue her wrong. Like you hadn't met her two dozen times before, four times each year, in the good years. Every time the door opens your grandmothers act like they can't believe the other one still exists, like surviving is the biggest miracle and maybe it is. But the year Ada turned twelve, she made like you were someone brand-new, a boy she'd never noticed before.

"I'm Ada," she said, and you said, "Yeah?" careful to show that you noticed nothing new and couldn't remember the last time she'd come. Like some part of you hadn't been waiting for her, a little angry, maybe, at everything that keeps her far, at how many months had gone by between visits. She wasn't even through the door when she was out on the balcony, hands on her hips, acting as if you were her own appointed consulate of astronomers. As if your scope was made for her. It was dusk, next to night. The stars were playing tricks with the lights of West Berlin.

"Let me see it?" she said.

"What?"

She cocked her head to one side, like she was measuring you, like that mole of hers wasn't for kissing. "Everything," she said. "Everything you can get from your measly four-power."

"The air's rambunctious," you said, holding back, not touching her. Not touching her yet, because you were waiting. "There's nothing to see."

"Don't be stupid," she said.

"I'm not stupid," you said.

"The air is not rambunctious," she said. "Can't be." And she was so sure of herself, so pretending that you were brand-new in her life, that you had to kiss her.

Now when Ada comes she acts like she's a professor. She makes like she's researched every last centimeter of jumping the wall, everything it takes to be a hero—like she would do it herself, if she had to. Across a tightrope, she says. On a speeding train. In a stolen uniform. By way of a tunnel. In the trunk of a car, on the floor of a car, beside the heat of a car engine. Over the first fence and the next and the third, and past the mines and the twenty-two-centimeter-high asparagus grass and despite the dogs and in the middle of the night and across the river and in the basket of a hot air balloon stitched out of worn-down bedsheets. Four times a year, and sometimes less than that, she comes to your flat and stands there in the dome of night giving a little lecture on all the ways the wall's been overcome by people with less than you to lose. Her hair's whatever color she makes it. Her fingers are skinny as bone. She's cool in the summer and warm in winter. She's a girl who won't take no.

"I'm waiting," she says.

And you're listening to her. You're listening, and so is everyone else, and afterward, after Ada has spent the day she's been allowed to spend and the half-zone of night, you can think of nothing but her at the Eisfabrik on Köpenicker Strasse. You work the boiler house and the engine room remembering her kisses. You check on the cork between the walls and think of her slender weight on you. You write down the history as Alexander gives it—the old facts about Carl Bolle the Bimmel-Bolle man, who bought this place in 1893 and started making his sheets of ice three long years later. Carl Bolle ice went to breweries and pubs. It went out on the trucks with the dairymen. It went to houses before houses had refrigerators. It went to the men with the fish. Big sheets of ice, 1.5 meters long—that's what the Eisfabrik is famous for. Two world wars and a bunch of fires later, it's still turning running liquid into solid cold, and you're its newest apprentice. Alexander's your boss and your instructor. He's teaching you what he can about how pipes fit and how waters run, how cork insulates, how turbines hum, and all the time he talks you're picturing Ada, trying to remember which side of her face her mole had landed on.

Your future is plumbing, the Stasi say. Ada grinds the sole of her boot into the nubs of the rug and says you're aiming low.

SO36

*

I have a job, and it pays. On the best days, I hitch a ride on the back of Arabelle's bike and let her brown coat smother me like snow. It scratches my face as I squeeze in behind her.

"You're a whiff full of paint," she says, as I latch my hands beneath her ribs and above the small mound of her belly.

"No time for the lavender cure," I tell her. I'm already late as it is.

In the daylight her bike is a special sight—all those streamers of wool and the twin lime fenders, the baby-blue banana seat, the red handlebar bell that does a bad job of warning off traffic. I get all wrapped up in the wool and her hair. I wish I'd worn my gloves with the fingers. Another February freezer.

"You see Peter last night?" I holler forward.

She nods. Her rasta hair bounces crazy.

"He tell you he loves you?"

No answer.

"You tell him your part yet?"

She doesn't answer that either.

The vendors have been out since dawn. The caravans are busy, the little corner shops, the wood smoke piles, the minced lamb man and the dill weed man and the lady who sells the köfte. The air is a mix-up of factory bells and machine scree, the wide wallop of Arabelle's bike wheels across the cobblestone streets, the punk songs of Die Chaoten and the wind in the plane trees. The cars are pissed, the buses are crowded, the U-Bahn chinks on its rails. When we finally hit the platz, Arabelle takes her big booted feet off the pedals and conks her legs out straight, letting her coat catch the wind. She hee-haws like a donkey.

"Safe again!" she says.

"A miracle," I say. The sun might be out but it's cold as hell as we wobble and spin toward St. Thomas. Before the Berlin Cathedral got built this was the biggest church on both sides of the wall—a church to thousands of people—and even though it's six stories tall, the war has got nothing on it. When people call Kreuzberg a ghetto on the news, when they complain about all the smells and the mess and the squatters, I say you can't be a ghetto if you're standing this tall. You can't be a ghetto if right here with you are Arabelle and basil forests and zurna songs and artists plus a hippie minister who's come all the way from California to keep us pure and holy.

The wind picks up, blows the sound of my kids toward me. I drop my Adidas and drag them; Arabelle does the same thing with her boots. The bike swerves, then stops, and I'm off it in an instant—unwrapped from Arabelle's coat and streamers and hopping until I am back at land speed.

"Pick you up this afternoon?" she asks.

"I'm walking home."

"You sure about it?"

"Sure," I say. "Mutti has put me on errands."

"She must think you're Superwoman," Arabelle says. "Out all night, work all day, errands in the evening."

"She thinks it because I am," I say, not even smiling because it's true.

"Peace," Arabelle says, the donkey back in her smirk.

"And to you," I say.

She's off to the Köpi, where she works three days a week teaching German in secret to Turkish women in headscarves. "Earning them their independence," she says, like the rebel she is, the rebel she's made me. Later tonight she'll be out on the streets, riding her bike full of streamers. She'll be looking for Peter, her American boy, come all the way from a Pennsylvania college to help the Turks win their rights from this country.

Everybody has a plan, I guess. We're all on a mission.

*

The kids are at their table when I walk in—their eyes gigantic over their plumped-up cheeks and their hands sticky slicked with playdough, a fresh batch from Henni's kitchen. They're rolling the dough into snakes, tying the snakes into wreaths, putting the wreaths on their heads. The twins Aysel and Aylin can't stop standing and spinning. Henni doesn't stop showing them their chairs.

"Late again," she says, when she sees me shrugging off my jacket, unwrapping my scarf, tugging at my fingerless gloves.

"Sorry," I say. "I'll do cleanup later."

"No."

"No?"

"Not today. I need you to talk some sense into our fearless leader. He's over there in a psychic bind." Henni juts her two chins and her chubby fingers toward the end of the long table, where Markus, six foot three and string-bean skinny, has folded himself onto a toddler stool and is drumming the table with his blue-painted nails.

"What's he doing exactly?" I ask.

"Simmering," Henni says, her eyes rolling beneath drawn-on eyebrows. She fits Aysel back down into her chair and works the twins' hands into a bright ball of yellow dough. Aysel giggles when the dough glups, then Aylin starts, and now Savas yanks the wet wreath from the dark mop of his head and punches and pounds. "Making a dragon!" he says.

Meryem, already a flirt at four years old, gives Savas one of her missing-tooth smiles.

"What's he simmering *for*?" I ask Henni about Markus.

"I told him he couldn't teach the kids the protest songs."

"What?"

"From the Sixties."

"Why does he want to?"

"He says you can't be a proper citizen of Kreuzberg if you don't know your Sixties protest songs."

"Chrissake. Way to shut us down."

"Exactly. He'll get us all in trouble. Imagine if the kids came home sounding like German hippies. Will you tell him for me?"

"You haven't already told him?"

"He doesn't believe me."

I blow air into my hands, but they're still cold. I warn Aysel and Aylin from dancing on their chairs, tell Savas good luck with his dragon, smooth the static out of Brigitte's flimsy hair. I walk the length of the table and fit my rear onto a tiny bright-blue stool.

"Is it true?" I ask Markus. "About the protest songs?"

"It's not your business," he says. He doesn't open his eyes. He pulls his shawl around his shoulders, carries on with his fingernail drumming.

"It *is* my business," I tell him. "I work here."

"You only just started and you're only fifteen."

"I started in November and I'm almost sixteen. We can't go all radical with the babies, Markus. They're still learning how not to eat playdough. Plus, their dads will kill us."

He shudders beneath his shawl and uncurls the pencils of his fingers. He slowly opens his hooded eyes and sweeps a tragic look toward the dozen kids at the opposite end of the speckled Formica table—his would-be charges, his young radicals. He sighs, all bitterness. Everyone in the Kiez knows the sound of Markus's sigh, the flutter of his shawl, the big bird wings he hides beneath his too-tight shirts, where shoulder blades should be. Everyone also knows the size of Markus's heart, which is what keeps him here, at St. Thomas Day Care, where I took a job because we needed the money, and because Mutti couldn't stop me, and because I was all done with what the Eberhard Klein school was ever going to teach me. We're squatters, I told Mutti, and what we need most is cash, and then Mutti said, *You're too young to be so old*, and I almost said, but I remembered not to, that Mutti wasn't all that much older than I am now when she came home from the hospital with me. I almost said, *Somebody has to be old*. But I'm figuring out how I shouldn't hurt her, and besides, it isn't always her fault that she falls in love with the wrong men.

Stefan would never leave me like my father left Mutti. Stefan will do everything to have me. *Love proves itself*, someone said.

"Ada?" I hear Henni now, calling from the other end of the table. I look up at the clock—almost 10 A.M., story hour. She's putting the playdough back in its plastic box, except for the blob Aylin won't take from her head and for the dragon that Savas made, which he leaves to dry on the sill.

"So no protest songs today, right, Markus?" I say, as I stand up from the stool. "Promise?"

He presses his blue fingernails to his purplish eyelids. He sighs, the world's tallest disaster.

*

Savas says he remembers. Says he knows exactly where we left off yesterday in our story. "It's the fear one," he says, rubbing his belly with one hand, picking at a thread in the rug with the other.

"Does everybody else remember?" I ask, and there are ten nodding heads—black and brown and blond. Aylin doesn't nod because she's still wearing her playdough crown. Brigitte doesn't because she's sucking her three longest fingers. "Brigitte," I ask. "Do you remember?"

Her eyebrows quiver up, unsure. I open the big book to the very beginning and let the kids tell the story to me. "There was once a boy . . ." I start them off.

". . . who didn't know fear!" Savas says it twice—the first time in a whisper. He stands up again and raps his fingers against the tight drum of his belly, arching his back like he's nine months pregnant. He bites his lip, plops down once more, closer to me now than he was before and hooking his hand around my little finger, as if I'll need his strength to continue.

"That's right," I say, turning the page after he finally settles and unhooks his hand from my hand. "And so where does the boy go to find it?"

"To the thieves!" Aysel says. She puts her arms above her head, locks her fingers, holds the circle.

"And is fear there, with the thieves?" I ask the kids. I see Henni at the table, sponging off the playdough. I see Markus off behind her, watching the white day press against the room. He moves now, pushes the window up. He lights a long brown cigarette and blows the smoke out into the February weather.

"No, Miss Ada," the kids are saying, a chorus. Savas watches Markus, watches the window, seems suddenly distracted.

"Is fear in the cemetery?" I turn the page. They study the picture. They shake their little heads no.

"Savas?"

He turns back toward me. Squints his eyes a little. Says no. His cheeks are chubby and his eyes are round. There are spaces between his teeth when he smiles like there are spaces between mine.

"Is fear inside a lonely house?"

"No, Miss Ada." He makes my name last when he says it out loud. *Ada.* A name that could go on forever.

"Is fear at the bottom of the sea? On a boat in a storm?" I turn another page, and then another. The kids come close. They rock back and forth, pitching and falling, like they're about to be shipwrecked. But there's no fear on the sea floor and no fear in the storm, not for the boy in the fairy tale, the boy in the pages I'm still turning. Fear isn't anywhere. The kid can't find it. It's courage right here on these pages.

"What can you do?" Henni asked me when I interviewed at St. Thomas Day Care.

"I can tell stories," I told her. "And I can draw them."

Sometimes the hippie minister comes inside, to our school. Modern-Day Prophet, he calls me, because I see things, know them. I know that Mutti is sad, and that I can't fix it. I know that Omi will not forget the war. I know that Stefan will come and that I'll be ready. "Wall jumping's trouble," Mutti says, because she's watching. But I'm not afraid. I do not see fear. It's not with the thieves, it's not in the graves, it's not lonesomeness, and it's not in the storm. I keep turning the pages on the Turkish folklore.

"Brigitte," I say now. "Where's fear?" and she shrugs.

"Exactly," I say. "*Exactly.*"

I close the book and promise the kids more of the tale tomorrow. I turn and watch the white sun against the windowpanes and think of Stefan out there, Stefan with his shoulders so strong, his eyes so blue, standing high above his world and watching. I remember a summer day, three years ago, when the sky was pillow fluff. Stefan was waiting for us at the crossing, his grandmother beside him, his free hand stuffed behind his back. Joy is the silliest thing sometimes. Love is very funny. I ran to him and he bent to me. Kissed me on my nose, like a puppy.

"I have something for you," he said.

"Tell me," I said, stepping backward.

He took his hand from behind his back and it was there, like a shiny paper platter. A picture book of clouds in every color. A history of shapes. Cirrus and stratus and cumulostratus and every freakish and lovely combination.

"Secondhand," he said, blushing slightly.

"Brand-new to me," I said.

Omi had taken his grandmother's arm in hers, and they were off ahead of us, through the streets, toward the apartment and their history. I linked my arm into Stefan's, like we'd been married for years. "Take me to your balcony," I said.

"Hello, Miss Ada," Savas says now, and I look down and there he is, his arms raised high so I can pick him up and hug him. He extends his bottom lip and shrugs his shoulders. He paints a heart around my mole with his index finger.

FRIEDRICHSHAIN

★

You don't like it, but what's true is true: Their ears are everywhere. Between the walls, inside the phone, inside the static of the TV. The Stasi are downstairs, upstairs, on the street, in the schools, behind the flowers, in the Fernsehturm on the Alexanderplatz, in the U-Bahn, in the S-Bahn, in the wires, all along Köpenicker Strasse. If you're not extremely careful when you talk, the Stasi are at your front door and through, asking all the questions.

This is why—after your grandfather left, after he didn't come back, after it was only your grandmother and you in the three-room flat, inside the burgundy walls, on the upholstered chairs striped thin, the chair legs like twigs, the TV the size of a small pane of glass, the oven too small for a turkey, after it was only you two—this is why you taught yourself seeing. Seeing is silent and it doesn't leave a trace. Seeing is waiting for the sky to lose its turbulence so that you can scope the distance. Seeing brings the far close in and the dark to light. It's the ten billion stars, the galactic light, the buzz glow, the clouds that are frankly zodiacal. Seeing is boring the Stasi to tears. They watch you watching. You break no rules. They stand and they watch as you watch.

"I'll tell you a secret," you'll say to Ada when she comes.

"What?" She'll stand so close, smelling like coffee and strawberries.

"If you want to see something at night, you look just past it."

"Don't be stupid."

"I'm not stupid. Looking straight on makes a thing disappear."

"They teach it weird over here," she'll say. "Don't they?"

"Shhhh." You have to tell her. She is constantly forgetting.

She'll press her lips to your neck. She'll kiss your throat and bite your chin, take the words right out of your mouth, brush the light hair of your mustache with the red chip of her nail. Then she'll take your telescope in her hands and level it low for panoramic vision. Over the wall, over the Spree, past the canal, toward Kreuzberg. Ada prefers cities to stars.

"I'm trying to help you," she'll say. "Trying to *show* you."

"Shhhh." Inside, your grandmothers will talk, they'll remember. They'll whisper the years before, when there was no wall, but there were Russians. Your grandmothers had thought they'd seen the worst of it all through the second world war, but then the Russians came, and then the wall went up, and then the world was divided according to who was free and who was not, who would run and who could not, who escaped and who was murdered, or who was suddenly pregnant. There was a time when you had a mother. There was a time when you had a grandfather. There are the times that you remember and the times that you do not. All your grandmothers do is remember. They hold each other's hands.

"Look," Ada will say, when she comes. "Out there." She'll bring the streets into focus, the lovers along the canal, the big birds in the turrets of the old hospital, where there is art now, not sickness. She'll tell you to lean in, and you do. She'll say, "Listen, Stefan, they're playing our song."

"Who?"

"At the café. Listen."

"It's a telescope," you'll remind her. "A *telescope*. For seeing."

"You can't stay here," she'll say. "All right? That's what I'm saying."

"Ada."

"I'm serious, Stefan. I can't keep waiting."

"Can't or won't?"

She'll bite her juicy lip, touch the mole with her tongue, think on it. She'll kill you with thinking so long.

"Right now, can't. Someday, maybe, won't."

Your heart will drop from your throat to your toes every time she says it. Burn a giant hole straight through. Make it a bad day with Alexander at the Eisfabrik the next day and the next day and all the weeks you won't see her after that. "I thought you loved me."

"I do love you, and that's the point." She'll sway side to side, back and forth, in her Adidas sneaks or her beat-up patent-leather boots, one of its latches rusty and busted, one of the zippers going slack. "I love you so much that you're getting out of here."

"It's not that easy."

And then the lecture will come on. Ada Piekarz. Professor of Escape. And what can you do but listen? One after the other after the other, she'll tell her stories. Jumping, leaping, flying Ada. Like escape is one big circus act.

You'll let her go on, but you know how it is. You know how the jumpers have died: Bullets to the head. Nails in the feet. Volts up the spine. Lungs full of river. Falling from the sky. Chaos in the tunnel. Carried like meat. Caged like a monkey. In a holding cell. In the shock hands of the Stasi. In the teeth of a dog on a leash. In the bright light of the watchtower beams. When a herd of rabbits was watching.

You could counter everything she says—go story against story, proof after proof. You could tell the story you know best, about your own grandfather and how he went missing. About how you were only five when it happened and maybe it was all your fault. You spare yourself. You hold your tongue. You let Ada go on, being cocky. You let her say what she does, which is this: "Life's a big waste in the East. Life would be better with me."

You don't need Ada to tell you about waste. You don't need a soul to tell you how it feels to be stuck up here as man of the house with the woman your grandfather left behind. Your Grossmutter can't look at you. She can't love you. Your grandfather left you with a tube to look through, some mirrors, a mount and screws. He left you with your grandmother shrinking, playing the Black Channel all day long, like the good commie she never was and probably isn't. He left her dressing you up for the Young Pioneers and putting you out on the streets for Volunteer Sundays and making you wave at the parades from your window. He left her sending you out of the house singing that song you will always, until the day you die, hate to hear anybody singing:

Take your hands from your pocket
Do some good, don't try to stop it.

Your grandfather left her shaking.

The Stasi are close. They're always listening. Your grandfather is gone, and it's your fault. You see Ada four times a year, and by the way: You love everything about her.

SO36

*

By the time I get home the kitchen is dark except for the pilot light and the candle Omi burns, like that little bit of flame can warm her. I can see her hand, cutting through the light, stirring her coffee with yesterday's bread. I can see the soft hairs on her chin and the thin lines around her mouth, where she holds all her worry.

"Your Mutti's out," she says, and I guess that means Sebastien. Another man to try to love. Another heartbreaker.

I shrug and my bag slides to the floor. I dig out three steaming bratwurst sandwiches and set them on the table, letting the smell of the hot mustard fume. The crinkled aluminum paper catches the light of the flame.

"We should eat ours now," Omi says, like the conspirator she is, "while they're still hot." Suddenly the ridge of worry above her lip is softening. She slides her coffee off to one side and unpacks her bratwurst until the aluminum is neat and square, polished as a dish. "You must have known I was hungry," she says, biting in.

"You're always hungry, Omi," I say. Because she is.

"Thank the war," she says. She always says it.

"Good?" I ask.

"Delicious." She never swallows anything until she's chewed a dozen times. "We made it last." That's what she tells me. The frogs they boiled in heated buckets. The bark they pulled off trees. The chalk they ate that tasted like erasers. The candy the Americans had thrown from the skies. They made their food last through the worst years of the war and Omi makes her food last now. She sits there in her chewing silence, remembering how it was, going over the stories she has told me and told me. She was eighteen and her father had not come home from the front. It was the winter of 1946, and they'd been left—her mother, her sister, herself, the baby she didn't know she was having. Berlin was a city of smash, that's what she says. Seventy million cubic meters of rubble and the coddled afterstink of bombs. Berlin was shortages and ration cards, fake coffee, raisin bombers, and even the linden trees of the Tiergarten were gone, where she had chased big-winged birds when she was a girl. "Conquered and divided," she will say. "Hungry," she'll repeat. "We were always hungry. We made our meals last."

She gnaws into her bratwurst sandwich. She chews, a squishy sound. I wait for her to tell me something about right now, or back then, but she's too busy with the hot mustard on the warm rye to start a conversation. I remember the war for her—how they made marmalade from carrot stalks and honey out of pumpkins. How they traded American cigarettes for whatever they could find: a pair of shoes for a bar of soap, a bottle of beer for a pillowcase. How her own mother, in the room they borrowed, built a stove out of three bricks and some coal. The face of the building across the street had slid right off, and there were gardens planted on each floor, women sleeping with the turnips. In one room on one floor there was the stubble of a bush that would bloom lilac smells in the spring. That was the biggest mystery of all, Omi has said. The smell of lilacs in the spring.

"You know where Mutti is?" I ask her now.

She pretends she doesn't. There's glisten on her lips.

"You know if Arabelle's back?"

She gives me her don't-ask look.

I stand in the dark and walk past her to the square kitchen window that looks out over the thinnest part of the thinnest courtyard of our squatter's ville. Arabelle's bike is nowhere around, but somebody's stuck a German flag into Timur's empty box of basil, and the clothes on the line outside Gretchen's window are so frozen stiff with cold that they look like cardboard cutouts. It's blue and white and yellow out there, lit by flickering TVs and candles.

By the time I turn around Omi has finished. She has folded the aluminum into the smallest possible square. She's holding the candle like it's the center of a prayer, or like it's the only heat she'll ever have, or like she'll never forget that winter in Berlin, those walls without windows, those buildings without walls, those gardens growing out of living room carpets, that horse that somebody brought home for meat, that ox attacked by the pocketknives of widows. Like she'll never forget, worst of all, the day the mountain of bricks in the street exploded— the rubble falling back toward the sky, taking a small man with it, two kids. "Everything tossed like jacks," she has said. "Everyone coming down in pieces." An empty pair of shoes. Ten missing fingers.

"You have told us," Mutti will remind her.

"But it happened," Omi will say.

She holds her candle very still and nothing moves except the creep of worry and the glisten on her lips.

✳

It's late by the time Mutti comes home on the back of Arabelle's bike. I hear the ruckus of her, hear someone from an upstairs room calling "Shhhhh," and now the baby on the third floor is crying. Gretchen's face appears in the window across the way, beyond the frozen aprons. She's tied a scarf around her yellow curls. When she opens the window to get a better look down below, I hear the wheeling rise of the reed high in the song of a zurna. Another Turkish boyfriend for Gretchen, the tattoo artist who lives across the courtyard. Another rule half broken.

In the courtyard Arabelle presses her big face against my mother's small one. She holds her arm across my mother's shoulders, her wire-framed glasses snug in her dreadlocks. She wedges her bike against the wall with one hand, then helps Mutti forward. They move along, the two of them, like someone tied their legs together.

"I'm fine," Mutti is saying, her words slurred.

"Nothing to it," Arabelle tells her. One door clicks and there are echoes on the metal staircase. There's no sound, then the sluff of carpet shuffle, then the loose jiggle of the one-screw doorknob, and now they are here, Arabelle's face like cardamom and Mutti's pale as moonlight. The two chestnuts of Arabelle's eyes tell me to be quiet.

"We'll put her to bed now, won't we?" she says, her voice like the low strings of a guitar.

She's done this before. She knows the way. It isn't far, anyway, to Mutti's bedroom. "We're home now," Arabelle says, and Mutti agrees. She sits on the edge of her bed, obedient. She lets me peel away her gray felt coat, her scarf as long as the bedroom. Arabelle slips the boots from her feet. Mutti lies back and we pull both crocheted blankets to her chin. She sighs as if she's already asleep.

The kitchen is as dark as Omi left it when she blew out the candle in the jar. Now Arabelle takes her lighter to it and flames the wick and lets her face change colors above the yellow tongue of fire. She sits there tying the yarns of her hair into their Wildstyle, the flame going orange now, now purple.

"She was down at the canal," she finally tells me. "Too close to the edge."

"Why? Did she say?"

"Who's Sebastien?" Arabelle asks.

"Never met him," I say. *Never want to*, I think.

"I don't know," Arabelle says. "Really. She just kept saying 'Sebastien.' Like he had hurt her somehow, broken some promise."

I imagine Mutti out there, without gloves, without a hat for her head, walking along the icy water. I think about how she zags inside her sadness, how that is what sadness is: a zag. If she fell in, the Vopos would shoot her in a minute. If she fell in and sank, none of us would ever find her. She was born too thin, that's what Omi says. But there's more to her sadness than that.

"I have bratwurst," I finally say to Arabelle.

"I wouldn't mind," she answers. She moves the jar of light to the left, then back again, as if she is playing chess, or checkers.

I dig both sandwiches out of the oven, where by now they've lost their heat, and sit back down. Arabelle splits the aluminum wrap with the other end of her lighter. I unwrap my own slowly.

"Will you see Peter tonight?" I ask Arabelle.

Her mouth's full; she shakes her head no.

"You should tell him, you know."

"When it's time." She eats slowly, her eyes on the sandwich, and tells me about her day instead, about the Turkish knitters of Köpi. Every day the women come to the shop and knit, and every day Arabelle teaches them German. The sweaters get sold and the husbands don't know and stories get told and there are secrets. My own patchwork sweater comes from the Köpi, and so do both of Mutti's blankets, and also my pink and green stockings, my gray cabled tights, all of it smelling like dill and yogurt until you wash it once in the sink and hang it to dry on one of the lines that go corner to corner across the courtyard.

I listen to Arabelle talk, don't ask her questions. I don't press her for the facts on Mutti, even if she is my best friend and not my mother's. Arabelle's older than me by four years, and she's always keeping what she knows about my mother to herself. It mostly works out for the best.

I eat my sandwich, savor the mustard. It's the first taste and the last taste of a decent bratwurst sandwich. It's the heat that you get when the meat goes cold.

"You working tonight?" Arabelle asks me now.

I nod.

"You need the bike, you can have it."

"*Danke.*"

"You should try pumice," she says, about the flesh around my nails, all of it speckled and splattered.

She yawns and I see both rows of her teeth. I think of all she's doing for the Turkish women of Kreuzberg, who live in this part of Berlin like it's someplace borrowed. Like it wasn't the Germans themselves who begged the Turks to come here after the wall went up and the factories in our parts weren't suddenly starving for workers.

"Calling it a day," she says.

"Thank you."

She looks confused for half a second.

"For Mutti," I say. "For bringing her home."

"She'll get better," she says. "I promise."

"I don't know," I say. "She's always like this."

"Time," Arabelle says.

"You should tell Peter," I say.

"Yeah."

She stands and the light leaves her face. I hear Mutti's bed creak beneath her, hear nothing but silence from behind the door to the room where Omi sleeps. I fit the candle in the jar on the flat of my palm and walk Arabelle to the door.

"*Nacht*," she says.

"*Nacht*."

I close the door, run the chain through the lock. Put the candle on the floor, rearrange my cans of colors. I sleep a little before I go back out—find a place on the couch, hug the pillow. I think of Stefan and the feel of his arms around me. Everything solid. Everything safe. As if I'm eternal for that instant. Love is knowing that you're appreciated. Stefan appreciates me.

"My balcony princess," he says, when I'm there.

"Leave here," I'll say, "and I'll promote you to prince."

When I wake again it's nearly ten o'clock. I grab my bag, head out the door, clack down the stairs, hike myself up onto Arabelle's bike. I pedal, wobbly, across the courtyard and out through the open gate. I don't need to turn around to know what I know. My mother's up there: watching.

FRIEDRICHSHAIN

★

Leave it to Ada to bring them to you—folded in between her foot and boot, where the Vopos did not find them. She walked extra careful, she said; her footsteps never crunched. She stood in line with her grandmother and showed her papers, paid her marks, agreed to the terms of visitation, and all that time no one suspected what she was bringing to you—the newspaper stories, the proof of best escapes.

She read out loud. You calmed her down. She kept saying anything was possible and you kept telling her to mind her volume, to be aware, to remember the ears in the walls, in the hallways, in the balconies across the way.

"Shhhh, Ada."

"Listen, Stefan."

"Could you please," you said again, "be a little careful?"

"Could you take an *interest*?"

Her words sounded foreign against your words and you

wondered: How could one language be so different? How could one girl be so wrong and also so kissable?

There were all kinds of stories in the papers she brought. There was a list of best gadgets. Double-jointed ladders. Invisible string. Escapable coffins. Cars that run with only half of their engines. Flamethrowers. There were interviews with the escapees. There will always be a minor business in heroes.

"Where did you get these?" you asked her.

She made like it didn't matter.

"You're dangerous," you told her.

"You can be so smart," she said back, "when you're not so busy being stupid." She has this gap between her two front teeth, and one of those teeth is bigger than the other so when she smiles, and she only sometimes smiles, it's like two little surrender flags have been hung at different angles. You loved her that day more than any other. You loved her and you listened as she read, telling her over and over again to stop being so busy planning the end of your brown-colored existence. There were, you said, complications. There were problems with her stories. You asked her if she'd eaten. You asked her to go outside with you, hand in hand, and walk the park. You said you'd take her to one of the pubs and get her a sandwich and she looked like she thought you were crazy.

"I'm talking about freedom and you're talking about food?" she said.

"Aren't you hungry?"

"Are you serious?"

"Do you want some noodles?"

"Pay attention!" she said, shaking the sizz of her fluorescent hair, which is charged, electric. You wanted to reach for her but you made yourself wait. It had been three months and you'd missed her crazy and she was right there with you in her tight jeans and splattered sneakers, her little T-shirt with the silkscreen ruffle, and she wouldn't stop talking. "Kiss me," you said, and she wouldn't.

"Kiss me."

"Not until you listen."

"I'm listening." Her skin so sweet. Her flesh soft and high on her bones. Her body so close on the balcony where your grandmothers couldn't see you, beside the scope, which she was angling then, away from the sky, angling it toward Kreuzberg.

"Everything you want is there," she said, pointing to the canal and the church, the plazas and the crazies, the stretch of the wall that she has graffed just for you, her sacred trust. "And besides, I'm not waiting forever," she said. She wasn't keeping on like this, she said—striking the days between visits off that calendar of hers, standing in line at the station, trading her marks for your marks, hiking in with the bootleg videos, trying to remember the color of her mole in the last visit so that she could make herself seem brand-new again. She had so much to say. So much she wanted you to see. The Viktoriapark and painted trees. A kid named Savas who holds her hand. A bike that drags wool streamers. She said you have no business being happy with what you're allowed in the East. She said you do not know what happiness is.

"Happy is right now," you told her. Because finally, after all that, after you had not taken her to the pub, after you had only quickly kissed her, the moon had come up, a curved slice in the sky. The moon was out there and the moon was yours and she said—you won't forget it: "I need you. I need you to help me with Mutti. I need you to meet Arabelle and Savas. I need you to see what I've been making for you, what kind of artist I am. I need you to surprise me, Stefan, to show up sometime when I don't expect it, to leave a pot of flowers outside my door, to pedal for me on Arabelle's bike so I don't have to. I need you, Stefan. I need to be safe." She said it, and she was crying, and you remember every word she said, you play it over and over in your head, in the night, at the Eisfabrik on Köpenicker Strasse, at lunch when you sit with Alexander telling him what it's like to be in love.

"I need you, too," you told Ada Piekarz. "I need you for everything."

"Then prove it."

SO36

*

Everything I write on the wall has either happened or will. Take the bent knee and black boot that I have graffitied in shadow 3D. That's my symbol for Conrad Schumann, who was nineteen years old on August 15, 1961, just days after the East German Communist Party split this city with the silver thorns of a barbed-wire fence. Conrad was wearing his machine gun when he jumped the barbs. He was one of them, an East German border guard. He took a don't-look-back run and Terpsichored far enough, from there to here, to safety. Conrad Schumann took a flying leap. I took a fat cap and three Krylon aerosols. Did my fills left to right, used yellow for my highlights, left the drips. You can stand up close to the wall, in Vopos country, and smell the color. Or you can stand back and let Conrad Schumann's boots come for you. You can ride the freedom in his leap. That's how I wrote it. That is my style.

"Ta Da." I tag it that way.

Close by my Conrad, on the buff of a solid spray on my part of the wall, is Bread and Toilet. Another true story: Believe it. It's 1964, and Wolfgang Fuchs is digging through the slippery mud of the dark ground between a bakery basement and an outhouse. Sometime soon entire families of not-Communists will walk from the smell of old shit to the smell of sugar before the Vopos take the whole thing down with a sick display of machine guns. But for a while that tunnel was light, and that's why I wrote it in lime green and white, why I put a pair of wings on my loaf of bread and sprinkled some nice angel dust on my toilet. You don't need the self-satisfying interlocks of Wildstyle when you have a story to tell, all those letters so secret and squished that no one but you knows their meaning. You just have to pop your colors, plant your outlines, and hold the can straight up so that the dip tube sinks deep into the butanes and propanes.

I used the hollow-cone nozzle for the car escape story. I stayed very still and perfectly central to get my rounds right, my mists even. Horst Breistoffer, the hero of this getaway tale, would have wanted it that way. He would have liked how I write with my cans. He was a man of precision. He cut out the car's battery and its heating system—genius, right? He folded people into the emptiness, under the hood. He drove escapees nine separate times under the noses of the border guards, who checked big cars, not small ones, put mirrors on the ground so they could look up and see if anybody was tied to a truck's hard, bright bottom; they didn't bother looking at his kind of car, which was, for the record, an Italian Isetta. Horst Breistof-fer was betting on the guards' big-car prejudice, and he bet right until the tenth time, but I don't write about that. My wall's the wall of great escapes. I only write true stories.

Tonight it's blues and purples I'm misting, white dust. Tonight my red bandana is high on my nose, my hood is pinched, and my light's wedged in. I've shaken the Krylons hard, punched their noses, swapped a full cone out for a flat streamer, because I'm working the wall simple, in honor. I'm writing a burner. Horst Klein would like it this way—the acrobat on the high-tension cable. It's his sky I'm writing, his cable. His one hand and the dozen machine guns. His tightrope balancing East to West over the heads of the Communists. Simple like this could take an artist all night. I don't mind. When you're an artist, you don't.

"You'll catch your death of cold," Mutti tells me. "You'll get the Vopos in a snarl." But I know what I'm doing; I am fifteen, almost sixteen. I have been taking care of people all my life. I am out here because Stefan is coming—he will. He won't let me down. He almost promised. And when Stefan comes, I want to say, *This is for you; it's for us.*

I want to kiss Stefan up against the wall.

I want to press him into color.

*

I'm rounding the brick barrel of the church when I see the light in the day care window. It's three in the morning, black as pitch, and there's a soft snow falling, meaning: There should be nobody here. I stop the bike, hop off, untangle myself from Arabelle's streamers, and dig into the courier bag for my keys. The empty aerosols rattle around, my capable caps, my black book, which has gotten loose at its bindings. The keys are there, at the bottom of the bag, on their little pom-pom ring. They feel like chunks of ice against the hard bones of my fingers.

The snow is falling faster. The banana seat is frosting. I breathe in and out, and when I do, the air spots lavender and titanium—the paint settling into my lungs.

Whoever is in there has been in there for a long, dry time— there's no sign of snow or mud in the halls. Maybe Markus, I think, but I'd smell his cigarettes. Maybe Henni, but wouldn't I hear her? The only light in the hall is the crack beneath the door. I press my ear against it. Nothing.

The key in the lock pops it free. The knob rattles loosely. If someone's inside, they've locked themselves in. *It's probably nothing*, I tell myself. But then again, something says *Careful.*

"*Guten Abend,*" I say. "Hello?"

The lights are on. The room seems empty. There's snow blowing through the open window—a little crust of it along the low shelf of the back wall, where Markus will stand with his purple shawl on, puffing like a dragon. The blue and yellow plastic chairs are in their places at the speckled table. The nap-time pillows are in their pile by the rug. The smells are playdough, spilled juice, rag rug, dill, the hamper in the corner where we collect the warm, wet socks. When the wind blows and the snow skitters, the letters pinned to the ceiling by tacks make ripple waves above my head.

"Hello?"

I ask it; no one answers.

The bright lights, the locked door, the snow falling in through the window. *Hello?* I look behind me, toward the dark hall, then forward, toward that window. I turn my head like a periscope and concentrate my vision—slow and careful, high and low, into the bright and also the shadows. I see my own wet footsteps behind me, feel the slow run of blood through my half-frozen fingers, scratch the itch at my neck, under the bandana. It takes me a while before I see what I should have seen before—the hard clumps in the soft frost on the sill and along the shelf where hands have been, two feet. I drop my bag by the door, hurry across the room, and look out into the night, toward the fizz of snow that could any minute turn itself into a blizzard. There's the faint trace of footsteps out there, the ghosts of little feet running. There's a whole mess of scramble below the open window. There are no wet footsteps across the linoleum floor, no water stains on the braided rug. Whoever is here has been here for hours.

I turn back around—quick now. I feel eyes on me, something watching. I scan the room again and all is still, and then I see it: the black eyes and the puffy cheeks poking out from between the hand-me-down coats and scarves in the hook closet, the things left behind, or grown out of.

"Savas?" I ask.

"Miss Ada?"

If it weren't so strange and the light so mean, I'd be almost sure that I was back with the squatters on the tweed couch, fast asleep and dreaming. But I'm too awake to fool myself. And Savas is too frightened.

"Little man," I say. "What are you doing here, Savas?"

He's like a rabbit with a bad twitch. He's wearing a big black coat and polar bear jammies. His sneakers are loose and untied, dark and wet. He's sitting cross-legged and now he's rocking, back and forth—rocking and rocking, his teeth banging hard against each other. If I move too fast, he might go running—scramble back across the floor and up over the half-wall of books and onto the wide sill and through the window. If I don't find him a blanket, his teeth will crack from the percussion.

"It's late, Savas," I say, quiet, so he knows that he can trust me.

"I'm cold," he tells me, letting some air wheeze out of his cheeks.

"I'm closing the window," I say. "Okay, Savas? I'm closing the window, and then I'm going to come get you, and we'll talk. Okay, Savas? You okay with that?"

He nods, solemn. He nods, and he doesn't budge, just keeps on rocking, his teeth knocking, like somebody's playing the drums in his mouth, like this is what happens to little boys who hold on to silence too long, who are out in the night, out in the snow: How did he get here? What has happened? I walk slowly toward the closet, crouch a little, come closer. Markus's purple shawl is hanging from a hook. I pluck it off and bend to one knee. Savas's huge black eyes reflect the buzz of light in the ceiling fixtures above us.

"This should do the trick," I say, about Markus's shawl, which holds the smell of patchouli and smoke. Beneath the hems of coats and scarves, beside the boots and balls, the pogo stick, the Frisbee, I reach in and tuck the shawl over his shoulders and up under his chin like some enormous violet bib. He lifts his chin, then lowers it, like he's just remembered to defend himself from whatever thing he's run from. I loosen the bandana from around my neck, unzipper my coat. I pull the hood off my head and listen to the soft z-pop of static. And that's how we sit, Savas and me, way after midnight as the snow pings the glass, dangling threads of busted coat seams and scarf fringes dripping onto our faces.

"You have paint on your face," he says at last. "You have blue in your hair, Miss Ada." He puts his own hand on his chin, muffling his chatter. He covers his mouth. His eyes are burning.

"That's because I have a secret," I tell him, my voice a whisper, as if someone else could hear us. "Do you have a secret, too?"

He pushes his bottom lip out, squeezes his eyes, pokes his longest finger into one ear. "I think so," he says.

"Can you tell me?"

"No." He's sure about it.

"Do you want me to tell you my secret?"

"Uh-huh."

"My secret," I say, "is that I am in love."

His eyes swell and his teeth bang harder. "Love is a bad thing," he whispers. His rock is worse than it was, like he's riding some bronco, chased by wolves.

"Not always, Savas. Not really. Do you want to talk about it?"

"No," he says, and again, he's sure. He yanks the shawl over his face, and he starts crying.

Savas, Savas, Savas, sweet Savas. I hug his little body close and do not make him tell me.

✻

The snow brooms down from the tops of the trees that stand rattling their bones along the Mariannenplatz. It gusts—a white wave, an attack of crystals. "Keep your head down, Savas," I say, and the kid tucks his chin to his chest and holds himself steady on the bike's blue banana seat. He wears Markus's shawl like a cape and the gloves that I paint with. "Kottbusser Tor." That's all he said when I asked him where he lives. The heart of Little Istanbul in the riot of Kreuzberg on the right side of the wall.

It must be four in the morning, or close to five. The squatters are inside, the anarchists, the mosque men, the artists of Bethaniendamm, and all the shops along the Oranienstrasse are dark, the vendor carts locked up and shivering. Arabelle's bike strikes a wide skid down the whitened streets. The wool streamers are stalactites. There are little hills of snow up above my ears, where my hood blows back and can't save me. One arm around Savas, one hand near the bell, I'm pedaling fast, and I'm sliding. There's a lone taxi circling the streets. In its headlights the snow is white static.

When I reach the five points at the intersection, I brake slow, don't let the wheels flatten out beneath us. "All right, Savas," I say. "Hold on." He grips the handlebar more tightly. I hop off before we come to a full stop, keeping one hand around his belly. Now he sits on the bike like it's his own show pony, wearing the snow like a helmet.

It's bunker housing here—long parallels of concrete, the steel plates of satellite dishes, a mess of underground rails and overground rails and empty bus stops and tea rooms, kabob restaurants, kurdan cups. It's everything that's happened since the wall went up and the Turks came in to do the jobs that the East Berliners couldn't get to. They call them *Gastarbeiter*— guest workers—but they mean the farmers who come from Anatolia to clean our streets and build our buildings and sit with our old and eat their own bulgur wheat. They mean prayer rugs and headscarves and chickpeas. They mean women who hide themselves behind their burqas and girls who marry their cousins and little boys like Savas who are born here but don't belong here because with the Turks in Kreuzberg it's always temporary status—has always been temporary status since October 30, 1961, when the two countries signed the Recruitment and Procurement of Foreign Workers Treaty. In their own home country, at brand-new recruitment centers, the Turks were lined up, nearly naked, to prove they were healthy. They were given tests to prove they had skills. Then they were put on trains or planes and sent far from what they knew to a country, my own, which gave them crude housing and put them to work in factories for nearly nothing and without rights. We're not supposed to know what goes on behind those doors, but I've heard things. I'm not supposed to be here with Savas, but here he is beside me, my warrior boy on my best friend's bike, trying to be brave and fearless.

Is fear here?

Yes, fear is here. But I don't ask the question.

"Where?" I ask him instead, looking up at the faces of the bleak and endless buildings. But this kid is still not talking—this boy who ran all the way from Little Istanbul to old St. Thomas in some dark hour, his polar bear jammies going soggy to his knees and his big coat sliding off his shoulders, its lining smelling like beans. We read the fear book together, or at least I read it to him. We sat on the floor of the closet, all hungry and wet. We turned the lights off when we left, locked the door with my key, went down the hall, got on this bike, rode through the snow, ten centimeters now. It's not that it's far. It's that it is another country. I don't speak the language here, and Savas won't explain. The sky is growing lighter behind the snow.

"Savas," I say. "You're going to have to tell me." But he shakes his head no, and in the glow of a nearby street lamp I can see that he is crying. Big silent tears, like drops of rain streaking a window. *Henni would know*, I think. Henni the registrar, the administrator, the head teacher, the playdough maker. Arabelle could find out, Arabelle the hippie translator. All I am is me, almost sixteen years old, with a borrowed bike and a bag of caps and aerosols, my lovesick mother wearing herself thin watching for me through her suffering window.

I could keep on pedaling, but where? How far? I could turn around, follow the long white skid back to the Mariannenplatz, past the old hospital and the white-frosted birds in the turrets. I could key us back in to St. Thomas Day Care, or I could turn, go the other way, take Savas to Mutti and Omi, coffee and bread, candles burned down to their last centimeter of wick. I stand at five points looking three ways, my eyes blurring with snow, my feet like two chunks of the Arctic. I give the bike a nudge and it dips before it steadies.

"Hold tight, little man," I tell Savas.

The taxi circles again, a cat on a prowl, wicking its long tail of steam, and I'm shivering now, biting my lips, wishing Savas would tell me where he lives—which concrete room, which satellite dish, which place he's run away from, why. I push the bike harder but the snow fights back, and now Savas turns and gives me a black-eyed look, like he feels my fear, like I'm breaking my promise. *Nothing to be afraid of.* I yank my hood back, blow heat into my hands. Savas looks up and down the snowy splatter of me and puffs his cheeks into that smile.

"Now you're pink and blue and white, Miss Ada," he says.

"And you're a king," I say, my lips blue, my teeth chattering. "A hero."

He forgets, for a half a fraction of a second, that he's escaped from somewhere, that he's been crying. I lift the shawl from his head and shoulders and flap its snow onto the ground. I wrap him up again and suck in the air and turn the bike back around the opposite way and keep searching for his home.

Past the concrete flats and the shallow dishes. Past the dark Turkish markets. Past the silver vendor carts and the mosques in the cobbled alleyways. Savas rules the banana seat and I rule the end of night beside him. Except: I don't want to rule. I don't want to be the one who is supposed to have the answers. I don't want to be by myself out here with a little boy, and it will be dawn soon, and everything hurts, and every part of me is tired, and I don't have a good plan. We go in circles and the snow falls hard, and my lashes are crusted, and the purple scarf is no shield. And maybe that's why I don't see what happens next at first, or why I can't understand. Maybe that's why I'm not ready when it happens. But something's coming— big and frightening—a giant bird, maybe, or a monster. It runs down the sidewalk, flapping its big black wings. I stop short in my tracks. My heart is pounding.

"Savas?" it calls.

It hurries like a terror down the long bent road, through the shadows. I lock both arms around Savas, let the bike fall— its lime-green fenders in the snow, its iced seat, its rusted chains, and bright red bell. I have nothing on whatever this is—nothing, and I wonder—split second—what Stefan would do if he could see me now, if he is watching through his scope, if he will jump the wall and save me. I run toward where Savas and I came from, over our own wide marks. Savas is heavy. My boots are slipping. But I'm running.

"Ahn-neh," Savas keeps saying, looking back toward the big black thing.

"Ahn-neh."

"Ahn-neh."

But I'm not listening. I'm just running, keeping us safe, until finally some of what the kid says rushes in. "No, Miss Ada," he's saying now. "Stop. That's my mama."

"What, Savas?"

"My mama."

"That?" I stop in my tracks, skid a little in the icy snow, turn. The black bird is still after me. The black bird is a burqa.

"Savas!" it says.

"Ahn-neh!"

"Savas?" I say.

"My mama!"

He wrenches out of my arms and down onto the street and plunges toward it. It happens just like that—in a second, in the snow. I see her eyes above the veil, dark and nearly swollen shut.

"Are you all right?" I ask, as Savas buries into her.

But she doesn't understand my German.

"Somebody beat you," I say. "Somebody did. Who?"

But she bows, lowers her gaze, doesn't understand me, or maybe she does. Savas clings to her like a spider.

"Ahn-neh," Savas says again. She shifts him up higher, onto her hips. She reaches one hand to the veil across her lips and places a finger there, like a big shush sign. Then she turns and runs with Savas in her arms, and I know at once that I have done the wrong thing. I know that I have lost him.

"Savas!" I call, my hands at my mouth, my heart in my throat.

FRIEDRICHSHAIN

★

Whenever she comes she has to go, and then the bubble pops. And then nothing's pink, everything's brown. Brown and that burgundy that clings to the walls and the color of those chairs, which is nothing. When she's gone it's your life as it is. Your Introduction to Socialist Production. Your Technical Drawing. Your training and the certificate that's coming. The Eisfabrik where you apprentice for the life your comrades have picked out for you. Augers. Wrenches. Washers. Cutters. Grinders. Ice. Get the hang of it. You'll be a fitter. You'll cut and thread and hammer to spec, assemble and secure. You'll lubricate and heat and steam. Pneumatic and hydraulic. You were a champion swimmer once, a Spartacus athlete. But then they decided what your future is. They chose a track and a career, and now you're it.

"Think about it," Ada will say. "You're good at this."

"Good at what?"

"At pulling through."

But they're not training you for the escape carnival—not on Köpenicker Strasse. They're training you to endure. They're training you for a thousand marks a month, which buys what you and Grossmutter both need as long as you stay two corners short of the important-customer grocery stores, and by the way: Even if you have the cash to buy a car, you'll still have to wait a lifetime for a Trabant, which is practically the only automobile they sell to ordinary commies. It takes them forever to manufacture a Trabbi, and when they finally get around to making yours, all you have is a lousy two-stroke engine and a tin can of a car that spits noxious fumes.

The stars are yours. The stars and how you see. Gas clouds and reefs and nebulae. Spokes and spirals and twilight steam. Amateur, Ada told you once, is another word for love.

Who is going to blame you for wanting to believe?

Your grandfather disappeared. Your grandfather left and he didn't send for you, didn't finish the job, didn't get there. No ashes, no ceremony, no news, no proof, nothing. Once the Stasi started showing up, the Stasi were everywhere. Your grandmother went from regular old to ancient. She went from small to the size of a breadcrumb bird. She started hiding photographs beneath her bed, talking to people who weren't there, tacking posters of Lenin to the dining room wall, crying when she was frying the bologna. She turned the lights out at night and the Black Channel on. She hung your flag and the flag of the Union and grew an ugly old hitch in her neck: too much saluting. "Stop saluting," you said. Remember? You said it. She said, "Sing me that song," and you sang it.

Take your hands from your pocket
Do some good, don't try to stop it.

"*Guten Morgen.*" To the man in the Lada. "*Guten Morgen.*" To the gray overcoat across the street. "*Guten Morgen.*" To the skinny lady behind her *Neues Deutschland.* "*Guten Morgen.*" To Lenin on the dining room wall.

Ada brings you Pelikan ink pens and *Pop Rocky* magazines when she comes—smuggles them in, extra crafty. She traces your constellations with her fingers. She stands close beside you and even in summer, her skin is the perfect kind of weather. You show her the skies, she shows you her city—her Spree, her church spire, the signs on her shops where they sell duplicate versions of the exact same things, and also leather jackets. She shows you Arabelle out there somewhere. She shows you the idea of a boy named Savas. She changes the color of her mole and stares at you hard with her huge mineral eyes. She shakes her head of fluorescent pink. She puts her hand on your hands, her lips on your neck, she breathes and you smell paint.

She says, "I'll wait, but I won't wait forever."

And it absolutely kills you.

SO36

❋

"You're late," Henni says.

"I know," I say. "I'm sorry."

"You're late, and good Jesus Lord, you're a mess. What happened?"

"Sorry, Henni. Really. I'll make it up to you." I stare at her, hurting. Stand there on feet that won't thaw. My knees hurt and my butt and my arms. My back and my shoulders thanks to the push through the snow. I leave Mutti's old scarf in a knot at my neck. Keep the knitted cap on my head, my jacket zipped, my hands in my gloves, scanning the room for Savas. I smell like chickpeas to myself, old hummus. I have a spike of hurt in my head, a shiver in my bones, something hot behind my temple. Markus is over by the wide windowsill, looking blown about by wind, staring at the book in his hand. No Savas.

"What the hell is going on?" Henni asks, turning her back to the kids and to Markus.

"I'll tell you in a second, okay? I promise." Henni has blue eyes with enormous black pupils. She has fat little lashes that look like broken pencil stubs. She studies me and I half study her, then look past her, once again, toward the long, speckled table. The twins are side by side, four wide crayons in Aysel's fist, a spot of green on Aylin's nose. Dominik is sucking his thumb, arranging paint pots. Daniel's fingers are slimy with glue. Meryem's thinking, her chin perfectly balanced on the points of her delicate fingertips, and I know that she's thinking about Savas. The table itself is like some dumped-out bottom drawer—paints, crayons, brushes, markers, triple-wide popsicle sticks, construction paper, felt squares, zigzag scissors, the pipe cleaners that Meryem thinks are caterpillars. "They aren't alive," I always tell her. But she screams when they come near her.

There'll be a show, I realize, of some sort. The kids are making stick versions of themselves. It's all very abstract, and I don't understand, and there isn't time to piece it together.

"You look like you slept in a zoo," Henni says.

"Savas is missing," I say.

"I know," she says. "I called his house. Nobody was at home, I guess. No answer."

"We have to talk," I say.

"What's going on?"

"Not here, all right?" I glance toward the back of the room, the wall of windows, the deep sill, where Markus is hovering. "Markus," I call out. "Can you cover for us?"

"What," he asks in his moody best, "do you think that I've been doing?"

✳

"You're sure," Henni says now, after staring at me for what feels like an hour.

I nod, gnawing the splattered cuticle around my little finger, where the paint leaked in last night. My gloves are warming on the heater. My jacket's unzipped. There are heat prickles inside my cap. It still hurts in every bone. I stop my teeth from chattering.

"He ran all the way here, by himself, and climbed through a window." She tells me what I've just told her, in the same order I told it, every word measured and slow, like that will change the percentage of truth. She's old, Henni, like fifty or something. She has short legs and a wide middle. Her eyes are so blue they're almost violet. She had a boyfriend once, calls him Ancient History. She wears yellow canvas shoes and brown corduroy pants, that beat-up, rust-colored apron. These kids are her life. She's never had a runaway. She's refusing to believe it.

I remember something she said to me on the first day I started: The kids are only on loan to us. We screw up, and they vanish.

I give her a steady, unlying look and nod again. "He must have known the window would be open. Must have noticed Markus sitting there smoking. Markus does it, like, every day. Savas is smart. He remembers."

"Ada, he's five years old."

"Henni, he was here. All right? He was here. He was hiding in the closet." My voice ricochets off the thin kitchen walls, the silver refrigerator, the tiny oven, the two sinks, the faucet, the pantry shelves, the Dixie cups, the tubs of playdough. I start again, quietly, as composed as I can given the way that I feel, which is lousier than ever, and worried. "He was here and he was afraid. He was running away from something."

"And why were you here again, Ada? In the cold, in the dark, after midnight?"

"I was taking a ride."

"A ride."

"On my bike."

"I didn't think you had a bike."

"On my *friend's* bike, Henni. What does it matter?" I've torn the cuticle down to the flesh, popping a ruby of blood— bright red and wet as polish. I feel Henni's eyes on me, like I've done something wrong, like it is my fault Savas ran away, my fault that I found him. Beneath the cap, my hair is smashed and hot, and on my lip an old yellow mole is melting. I watch Henni through loose strands of sunshine, wonder when Markus will come in here and stare down his thin nose and declare that his shawl has been stolen.

"Are you sure it was his mother—that woman on the street?"

"Who else would she be?"

"I don't know, Ada. I'm finding this hard to believe." In the big room around the corner from us the saucer feet on the chairs are squeaking and the kids are growing noisy. Dominik is fighting for a pair of scissors with his favorite word of all time: "Mine." Markus is telling Aylin that it's time and Aylin's turning "No" into a song. Now someone is running—the *splat splat splat* of their feet across the linoleum floor.

"Savas is missing," I say. "That's what I know. And he was afraid. And we should find him. We have to, Henni. You have his address, right?"

"You know how it is, Ada. We're not exactly welcome guests in their wedge of Little Istanbul. Besides, if she'd wanted your help, she would have asked for it. If this all happened the way you say that it did."

I brush the pink out of my eyes, give her one of my looks. My eyes blur. I focus. "She doesn't speak German, Henni. How could she ask me?"

"But she ran. That says enough, doesn't it?"

The bright pop of blood near my nail has smeared. The kitchen smells like baked wool. Markus has found his guitar and he's strumming, circling the room. I catch a glimpse of him in the silver face of the refrigerator. Dicle, a dark-haired kid who joined the class a month ago, is parading after him, a pipe cleaner up against his mouth like a zurna.

Now Meryem's up, and Ece with her, and when Markus hits the la-la chorus, the room echoes with the sound of kids singing pop English—German kids and Turkish ones, the wrong words and the right ones, Markus out in front, trailing patchouli instead of his shawl. Savas, I think, should be leading the band. Savas should be here, but he's not, and I shouldn't have let him go last night. I should have run after his mother, forced her to explain, with her hands, maybe, with Savas's help: *Who hit you? What's happened? Where are you taking him?*

"They live by their own rules," Henni says now. "By their own customs."

"But Savas is our responsibility."

"I know," she says. "I know. I'm thinking."

✿

Mutti is waiting. I don't see her at first, pitch my bag to the floor, scrape out a chair, unwrap my vendor-cart sandwich. I close my eyes and lift the sausage to my face, give my nose a little steam bath. I try to think, but my head's all cloudy, my bones are hurting, the atmosphere of me is clammy.

"What's going on?" I hear her now.

She's thin as she is. She leans against the open door that connects her room to the kitchen. Her tight jeans are too loose. Her red socks are fuzzy. Music bangs in from the flat above— that red balloon song with the war words, Captain Kirk and fireworks. The singer's voice is high and sweet. The drums are full of echoes. Now from downstairs someone turns the Beatles on. We're caught in between.

"Nothing's going on," I say.

"You didn't come home," she says, "until dawn."

I lift my shoulders, drop them, think of Arabelle in the kitchen, explaining again: *She was down by the canal.* Think of how we laid her in her bed, the sweet sickness of drink on her breath, the blankets to her chin, her heart all broken again. Sebastien. A painter from France, Omi has said. And now a part of my mother's ever-tragic history. She'll get better, everyone says. But I don't know what better is.

"The art was bitching last night, Mutti," I say. "I stayed out late to finish a graff."

"Is that the truth, Ada?"

"Mostly." *Mostly* itself is a word that doesn't lie.

My little finger throbs where the cuticle ripped. There's a strip of burn on the roof of my mouth. If I tell Mutti about Savas, she'll flame out like the end of a match. "Protect your mother," Omi says. My job, since the day I was born.

Mutti leans away from the door and pulls a kitchen chair toward her. It hardly creaks under her weight. The purple question mark on her white T-shirt sits crooked on the small shelf of her breasts. The polish on her nails is chipped. The line of silver-pink scar across her inner wrist glistens like half a bracelet. It's nothing, she says, when people ask her about it. She's lying again. That scar is proof that Mutti has what it takes to survive herself.

"You don't think there will be trouble," she asks, "living like this?"

I don't answer; how can I answer? This is Mutti, sad Mutti, who spends half her time not even living. I force my sandwich down, fist up the silver wrap. Downstairs the Beatles are turning over to Bob Dylan, and upstairs the balloons are gone, and I'm here with my secrets and Mutti with hers and Omi behind the brass lock of her hollow-core door.

"Can't you talk to me?" Mutti says. "Please?" She lifts a hand to my right cheek and then presses it to my forehead and suddenly I'm so extremely tired and much too dizzy and stupid helpless and I'm slipping, wanting to tell her everything. About how it felt to push Savas through the snow at night. About the monster bird that was the kid's mother. About how much I miss Stefan, how I don't know for sure what he'll choose to do, how I'm not really a Professor of Escape, just a girl in love who will not let her own heart break in family style. I'm a girl rejecting my genetic history. I'm a girl who lost a boy in the dark of Kottbusser Tor. I close my eyes and I see snow. I open them and a salty tear makes its way to the corner of my mouth.

"You're warm," she says. "You have a fever."

"No," I say. "I'm fine." But my eyes are closing and it's hard, really hard, sitting here pretending I'm fine. "I just need a minute," I say, and maybe a minute goes by, or ten, but now I feel Mutti's arms around me, feel her thinness lift me, her half-strength float me like one of those sad, red balloons.

"Here," she says.

"I'm fine, Mutti," I mumble. But I'm not, and she's here— thin and worried, suffering like she does, leading me away to the couch. She helps me from my jacket, unpeels the cap that is glued to my head. She leaves me and then she comes back, and I feel her lift one of my arms as she tucks in the little bear I slept with when I was a kid. The blind bear with the vest of buttons and the two rectangular teeth. Mutti made the bear, with socks and felt and thread. Mutti made it when she was young, before living like we do became too hard.

"I'm fine," I insist, but I'm cold inside and hot everywhere else, and when she touches my head again with the tips of her fingers I feel the prickle of it low in my spine.

"Mutti?"

"You need your rest."

"Can you tell them?"

"What?"

"To stop the music?"

"Oh, honey."

And now she sits there, on the far end of the old couch, rubbing my feet with her fingers. Everything is upside down and reversed.

"Close your eyes," she says.

I'm floating.

I dream red balloons and fighter jets, fireworks and squadrons. I hear Omi in the kitchen, talking; feel Mutti get up and sit down and get up and sit down; and here's John Lennon in a swimsuit and Ringo Starr with a drumstick microphone and Omi tiny, dancing. Omi pressing her hand to my forehead. Omi leaving her hand behind.

"Omi?"

"Shhhhh. Sleep."

Ninety-nine red balloons. Ninety. Nine. I write the number onto the sky. The sky is smacked with graffiti. "Look," I say, and Stefan's here. He has his hand on my head.

"Stefan?"

"Amateur," he says.

When I open my eyes it's dark. When I open them again I'm high in the sky in a basket, a plume of fire beside me. Flamethrower. Gas burner. It is working. We're escaping East Berlin—all of us and Stefan, too, in a hot air balloon as wide as the city's widest building. We're high above the silver teeth and spires, the sausage men, the tin can cars. We're high, and the river is running. The river and a boy with coal-black hair—a purple shawl flying out behind him, trailing the smell of patchouli.

"Ada?"

"Savas?"

"Shhh, Ada. Shhh. It's just a dream. Please. Have some water."

"Omi?"

I reach but she's far. I lean but she's there—on the fifth floor of a bombed-out building, no walls. The two orange frogs on her shoulders are hiccoughing words; the words are neon. Behind them an orchard grows through the low bowls of lit chandeliers, and past the orchard the city is burning. "You'll be all right," Omi is saying to the frogs on her shoulders, to me. "It's nothing," she says. "It's just a fever."

"Mutti?"

Crackers and soup. "Just a little, Ada. Good."

My eyes are like fishhooks. My words are like cotton. My city is no walls and neon frogs, chandelier bowls tipping soup. I feel something cool across my face, and then, for a long time: darkness. A thin sheet yanking and pulling. I hold on to my hair. It is pink.

Savas is here, like a spider.

Stefan is coming.

FRIEDRICHSHAIN

★

You have to wait for the right time. You have to wait because you know, because you have done your own research, because you have made your own lists, because there have been failures.

For example:

★   Roland Hoff, from trying to swim the River Spree with his briefcase at his chest. They shot him as he swam.

★   Olga Segler, eighty years old, from heart failure and spinal crack the day after jumping from her second-floor apartment. Because she missed her daughter.

★   Dorit Schmiel, twenty years old, shot in the stomach, treated like a hunter's catch. By her hands, by her feet, they dragged her bloody. She didn't finish dying for a while.

★   Klaus Brueske, from driving his truck across the border at top speed, border guard bullets to his head.

★ Christel and Eckhard Wehage, who killed themselves after their hijack-a-plane plan failed.

★ Horst Kutscher, after he'd already slid beneath the barbed-wire fence, after he'd already started along the security trenches, when there were only twenty-five meters left to freedom. Horst Kutscher. They shot him in the head.

★ Marienetta Jirkowsky, who was only eighteen, who had climbed the ladder, the final obstacle. Who was stepping East to West when they shot her.

★ Paul Stretz, and do you want to hear this? One hundred seventy-six bullets were fired.

★ Karl-Heinz Kube, who was in the death strip, who had bought his wire cutters at the Konsum department store.

★ Dietmar Schwietzer, who was eighteen years old, who was running, who was thirty meters from free. Of the ninety-one shots they fired, one hit him in the back of his head. They couldn't be worse at what they do, or more effective.

★ Giuseppe Savoca, six years old, who wasn't even trying to escape. Giuseppe was a kid playing with a friend. They were looking for the fish along the riverbank and he fell. The guards did nothing; they let him drown. He was six.

You have to wait. You have to be absolutely sure. Love is the biggest thing, of course. But there are other considerations.

SO36

*

"Shhhh, Ada. Look who's come to see you."

The middle cushion of the couch sinks. I open my eyes to the weight of it, to the wild springs of Arabelle's wilderness hair, to that little tattoo star that she wears like an apostrophe above one eye and that snake of a scarf at her neck. She stares at me through her wire frames, touches my face with her hand.

"That was some fever," she says before I fall away again and the only sound is the ping of snow crystals against the window, an argument on the stairs outside, the cry of a zurna. I am flying through the clouds of Berlin, the white cotton fog and wind, the upper lower troposphere. I am flying, and Savas is running. *Come back, Savas.* But out in the clouds is a balcony, and the balcony's a cage, and in the cage is Stefan. Something snaps and I lift my head and my head cracks.

"Arabelle?"

The room is gray, the windows are white, the snow pings hard on the glass. On the kitchen table, Omi's candle has burned down past the nub. On the other end of the couch, Arabelle sleeps upright, her head cocked, her breath coming out like steam through a grate, my feet on her lap. The door to Mutti's room is open. I see the edge of her bed, the quilt straight and unruffled. I try to read the clock that sits on the kitchen wall between the oven and the box refrigerator, but a shadow fattens its face. When I move the old stuffed bear beneath me squeaks. Arabelle opens one eye, rolls it my way.

"Somebody's back from the dead," she says, blotting a yawn with her warm, dark hand.

"God," I say. "What happened?"

She yawns again, shakes her head. She rubs the wet parts of her eyes dry, pushes her wire frames up the wide hill of her nose. "Flu," she says. "I guess."

"How long?"

"Two nights, honey. You've been one sick-girl mess. Spiders, Ada? Frogs? You've been spending too much time with those paint cans." She smiles. Her little baby teeth show. I try to count myself into whatever day it is, but I can't remember what day it was before, and now when I try to remember my dreams it's a landscape of stills—hyper tints, neon graffs, the color white, wind shears. I remember orange and pink. White sky and gray. I remember Savas. *Savas*. I think of Stefan.

Two nights?

"Shit." I sit up again, faster, straighter, ripping a clang through my head.

"Not so fast," Arabelle says, startling now, upright herself, as if she's only just remembered why she's here. "Look." She takes a glass from the table beside her. "Drink this, all right? You're dehydrated." She does a limber, big-rear scoot across the lame couch and helps me upright, lifts the glass to my lips. Swallowing water is swallowing knives. The stuff streams down my chin and neck, Wildstyle. It spills onto my shirt, the same shirt from two days ago, its collar sticky bothered.

"The kids," I say, choking on the clear stuff. I lean back, struggle with the crocheted quilt, but Arabelle keeps sitting there, anchoring me in. "And Henni."

"It's all right," she says. "We let them know."

"You did?"

"Your mother did, actually."

"Mutti?"

"Your Mutti and your Omi. To be one hundred percent honest."

I glance again toward her room. Nothing stirring. I hear a song from across the courtyard—Gretchen and her lover. Somebody's banging a pot on a stove upstairs. A couple of little kids are running. "Where is she, anyway?" I ask Arabelle. "Where's Mutti?"

"She's out with your Omi right now."

"Together? In the snow?"

"A miracle," she says, showing off her teeth again. I think about this, try to picture it. Where they would go. How they would be. Which would take care of the other.

"Where?"

"Don't worry about it," she says. "I'm here until they return. Your babysitter—tried and trusted, bona fide. Now what's all this stuff about Savas? What's happened?"

"I was talking about him?"

"Yeah, little girl. Like a lot, you were."

"When I was sleeping?"

"Taking a risk on this one, Ada, but I don't think you'd call that sleeping."

"What a mess."

"I'm waiting on it."

"How much snow?" I ask.

"Enough. They're fine."

"Where'd they go?"

"They'll be back."

"I've got to get out of here," I say. "I mean it." I fight with the quilts again, toss the bear to the floor, pull my fingers through my hair, pat my wet chin with the dry part of my shirt.

"You're a noodle, Ada. You're a mess. You're staying here."

"Does Peter know where you are?" I ask, giving her the eye. Try to one-up her, gain some arguing ground.

"Chrissake, Ada, will you stop asking questions?" She's annoyed and she proves it, snatches the bear from the floor, forces it back into the crook of my arm. "Sleep," she says.

"I'm not your practice child."

"Thank you very much."

"And by the way: I don't like you eavesdropping."

"Can't help it if you can't keep your mouth shut, Ada. Tell me about Savas."

"He's a kid."

"And . . ."

"And he ran away last night. Ended up at the church."

"And then . . . ?"

"I tried to take him home, but we got lost. Or he got lost. He wouldn't tell me where he lived."

Arabelle sits straight up; her wild hair springs free. She's watching me with a look on her face. I can't tell what kind of look.

"So then what, Ada?"

"So then we were kind of lost and we were coming home and it was late, almost dawn, I think—really late, but dark still, and snowing, and the bike wasn't liking the snow—and suddenly this lady appeared out of nowhere, like some big rubber shadow, and it was Savas's mother, and they were gone."

"Just like that?"

I snap my fingers, or I try, at least. I didn't realize that this flu of mine had stolen the strength from my hands.

"How do you know?" Arabelle says, very slowly, like I'm still too sick to understand, like I'm a little kid or someone stupid. "How do you know it was his mother?"

"Savas," I say. "Savas told me."

"God," she says, standing up abruptly. "Goddamn."

"You're freaking me out, Arabelle."

She paces the room, her hands at the small of her back.

"Could you, like, give me a clue?"

"Can't," she says. "I'm thinking."

"Think out loud."

"That wouldn't work," she says. "Wouldn't work at all." She plonks down on the couch, a wave bucking through. "We're forgetting about it," she says, "for now, okay?" She turns toward the window, and it's loud out there with snow.

FRIEDRICHSHAIN

★

When it snows your scope is silent. There's nothing to see but white dust. You stand on the balcony with the stuff to your knees. White then gray. Silent collapsing to hollow.

She calls your name over the test-pattern hum of the TV. She says, "Get back inside, Stefan. You'll catch your death of cold." She only says it once. She doesn't mean it. She doesn't mean most of what she says. She is afraid of flowerpots and thin umbrellas, formal jackets, new lapels, buttonhole pins, books that rattle when you touch them. "The Stasi are listening," she whispers. "The *inoffizielle Mitarbeiter*." Thrusting her finger at every corner of the room. She looks like a very old man, and not your grandmother. "We will be accused of *Hetzschrift*," she says. "Or of that other thing: *Schmähschrift*." Any word she can think of for the crimes she might commit: smears, libel, aiding, abetting. They have won their battle against her. She is afraid. She has been voided.

Sometimes you forget and you think that your grandfather is still coming back, and that when he does—when he clomps in from the street and climbs up the stairs and opens the door, takes off his hat, rubs at the shine on his head, puts his roots in and his arms out like a big old chestnut tree—he will not recognize her, will think somebody else moved in. You think that probably he won't recognize you either; and why should he, what's to say you're the same?

You're eighteen now. Your hair's grown thick, stayed curly. You're tall enough and brave enough to look him in the eye, to say, *I'm sorry.* You think you'll teach him the stars; that's how he'll know it's you. You'll show him what you have taught yourself to see. The gas tail of an asteroid. The boot prints on the moon. The razor whisk of arced blue. A distant pulsar. Antique starlight. The twin tricks to the telescope that he entrusted to you: aperture and ratio. You were going to be a cosmonaut, you will tell him. In honor of him, you were. You studied for it. You swam. You leapt. You did everything right, but they wouldn't let you. There were eyes everywhere, and their eyes accused you. Here are some terms that you've heard before: *Border jumpers. Deserters of the Republic. Grade one relative.*

"Did you really think that they'd let you into the skies?" your grandmother asked you, when you told her what it was you had wanted and what you would never have and how they had chosen your next day for you, your next month, your life: apprenticeship at the ice factory. Pipe fitter for the future. "They won't let you out of here. What good does dreaming do you? You're the grandson of . . . You're the child of . . ." She put her finger to her mouth. She wouldn't say it.

"She's just an old fart." Those were Ada's words when you told her what your grandmother had said. Two weeks later, you told her. It wasn't dinner yet, and your grandmothers were inside and you were out on the balcony, behind the curtain, where the old ladies couldn't see you. Ada was taking apples from her pockets. Pink liverwurst. Quality toothpaste. She was calling your grandmother an old fart and she was promising, planning, scheming:

"You're getting out of here, Stefan. I swear it."

"Try harder, Stefan."

Careful.

It's crazy, how much you miss Ada. How steel-gray dead the days are, how slow the clock ticks when she's not standing right here beside you. How easy she fits, under your arm. How large-minded and unsour her hands are. How when she talks about the kids she loves, the streets she walks, the köfte, the bike with the wool parts that fly, you want everything she is, even if there is no one word for it, no vocabulary for her where you live, and hardly any chance. If your grandfather couldn't make it free and back, then how could you? If your own mother got away and didn't come home to rescue you, then what's to say that bad luck doesn't run in your blood?

Ada will wait, but not forever. She sees hedgehogs, flood-lights, trip flares, control strips, signal fences, watchtowers, shoot to kill, and makes her decision: *No time like the present.*

There's no seeing through snow. There's no sound in the street, nothing but static on the TV. Out on the balcony, snow to your knees, the scope is silent. When it's cold and white like this you remember him and the day they put his box into the ground. It was an empty box because there was no body. There was no body because no matter how many times your grand-mother put on her coat and left the flat and walked all the way to the Department of the Interior, no matter how much she begged for an explanation, some information—*Where is he? What have you done? I want to see my husband's body. Please forgive me. Us.*—they sent her home with nothing. Empty hands. Bird claws.

You buried the idea of him, put that into the ground. It was 1974 and winter. It was before the slab wall with the smooth-pipe top. You went with your grandmother to the cemetery and stood opposite the pastor, and it was only the three of you and some birds shaking the snow off their wings and out of the trees and the West Berliners who had heard the ringing of the bells and had stopped and stood on their side, chins to their chests, hats off, fists in their pockets, and you could see them; they were right there, almost within reach—the people you didn't know and the people you did—Ada and her grandmother, Ada and her mother and her grandmother, Ada was so little there, a girl in a red wool coat. They stood where they were, crowded up against the wall, the bell song overhead, and the pastor talking loud so that they could hear his testimony about the man not in the box, the hole dug in the ground.

You tossed the first handful of dirt. You heard the echo splatter through the empty spaces of the empty coffin. Your grandmother offered a single rose. The pastor raised his hands, the birds flew, the snow fell. Later you would wonder what had happened to the rose, but now, standing here on the balcony looking out over the snow, you remember how you couldn't save him, couldn't save your grandmother, how two years had gone by since the last time you'd seen him, two years and all your unanswered questions. "Put it to rest," they had told your grandmother. "Put it to rest," she had told you. But her eyes were small black fish inside two big oceans, and she could barely keep her hand in yours, and you were the man of the house; you remember.

The bells tolled. The pastor lowered his hands. The birds flew back into the trees. The snow fell. And when you turned around there were only four now on the other side of the wall—Ada and her mother and her grandmother and another woman, too, in a bright blue coat. She had blond hair, long curls, blue eyes. She had a fern pressed to her chest, a shine on her shoes despite the weather.

"Tanja?" your grandmother said. "Tanja?" Her mouth fallen open and her teeth starting to chatter, a goose in her throat.

"Tanja!" She screamed it louder than any word you'd ever heard. She dropped your hand—tossed it away. She ran between the tombstones, beneath the trees, beneath the birds, beneath the snow that was flying again—ran right up to the edge of the first wall, the dividing line. Flying. Falling. Crash. But now Tanja was running, too, running away through West Berlin. The shine on her shoes was running. The bright blue coat. The hair like your hair—blond and curly. When your grandmother reached the wall—the signal fence, the concertina wire, the spaces in between, the division, the watchtower down the way, also above—there was no going on, there was nothing. There was Ada's grandmother reaching for your grandmother, but their arms couldn't touch, and there was your mother, running. It was the last time you would ever see her. It was the last time, and after that, the letters stopped, the small things she might send, the birthday cards. Her love.

"But where did she go?" Ada asks all the time.

"Free," you say. "She's free." And you hope Ada understands, takes it all in, does a little math on the bigger picture. You wish that she would. You leave or you stay. You're free or you're not.

There are always consequences.

SO36

*

"It's good," Omi says. "We already tried it."

"*She* already tried it," Mutti says. "*I* said we should wait."

I look from one to the other, each of them small in their own way and now, each of them glistening with white.

"How are you, Ada?" Mutti asks.

"She's better," Arabelle answers.

"Better," I parrot. Because the truth is that I fell back to sleep, that I'm not even sure what I dreamed and what I didn't. Maybe Gretchen came and went. There's noise past the doorway, down the long, dark hall. The black cat crying.

My mother's eyes are dark. It's like the storm has clocked her forward forty years. The crystal fur in her hair. The hard lines where the wind blew in. She's left her boots by the door and there's a lake of melt beneath them. The tip of her nose is the first edge of a flame. The skin beneath her eyes is purple shadows. She sits at the ridge of the couch with her coat zippered on while Omi, at the table, stirs the pot. Omi uses the splinter of an old wooden spoon—bangs it around like she's playing a drum. Now she jacks the whole thing up with her tiny hands and brings it to me so that I can see. Cabbage, leeks, potatoes, onions in a chunks-of-parsley vegetable broth.

"Henni made this?"

"While we waited," Omi nods. The carrots look like orange eyes. The whole thing smells like pepper. Omi carries the pot back to the table, her elbows out like pointy weapons, her knees a little wobbly with the weight, and I try to picture my mother and grandmother walking through the mess of Kreuzberg, the pot of Henni's *Eintopf* between them. The snow falling down and the steam rising up, putting its heat on their faces. I try to think of what they would say to each other. I cannot think of a thing.

Mutti unzips her coat to the halfway mark and stands on the fuzzy rug in her fuzzy socks. Finger by finger she peels away her gloves, then pulls her hands through the crystals of her hair until the color comes back—the black that is almost magenta. Now she turns and helps me up, too, lets me wear the quilt around my shoulders. She leads me to the kitchen table and sits me down. The chair is a Goldilocks chair. It wobbles.

"Arabelle?" Omi pulls out her chair and seats herself, like royalty in a hurry to be served. She pulls the collar of her black turtleneck up past her chin, gives me one quick look, closes her eyes not in prayer but in impatience. Behind her Arabelle is digging. Through the one cabinet, crooked on its hinges. Through the drawer, which sticks when you pull. "Aren't there bowls?" she asks at last, but there are tea cups and a Garfield mug, three plates, two saucepans, one spaghetti strainer, one rusty cheese grater, five spoons, four forks, two towels, a plastic measuring cup, a garlic press, a bright red ladle, a silver measuring spoon, and three knives that are good for butter, maybe, but only if the butter isn't cold. It's all my mother got out alive with—the kitchen stuff and also the bear and a trunk of clothes for us both. It was the second time she'd had to run. "Bad taste in men," Omi says. "Born unlucky," Mutti says. I don't know if my father was luck or not, but I do know this: Mutti's still walking the canal late at night. Walking too close to the edge.

"All right," Arabelle decides now. "This is it." She slides the saucepans onto the table, the Garfield mug, the broadest teacup. She ladles in and we wait, Omi's eyes too big in her face. Mutti shakes her shoulders out of her jacket and laces the bones of her fingers.

"To Henni," Arabelle says, when her ladling's done. One saucepan to Omi and one to me. Arabelle keeps the teacup.

"You sure?" Mutti says, unlacing her finger bones and offering a Garfield swap.

"I like what I've got," Arabelle says. She balances the eye of a carrot on a sugar spoon and makes like cheers, and soon Omi is slurping as if she's all alone, like we're not all sitting right here listening. Against the windows, onto the streets, into the courtyard the snow still falls, the brown dust that falls with the snow, the white and the brown that will spot the cow until the weather breaks. Stefan is out there far away and also close enough that I can feel him. Stefan is out there and I can't tell him a thing that I don't want the Stasi to read before Stefan reads it. "You write it in a letter and you give it to them," Stefan says. We're not giving one centimeter of him or me away.

"What you did is dangerous." It's Mutti talking, and even though I don't turn I know she means me, and even though I don't ask, I know Henni talked, that Henni would, because Henni says things. Henni talked while she made the soup, and my mother listened. Omi tasted. Mutti listened.

"Sorry, Mutti."

"Out at Kottbusser Tor at four A.M., with a boy on your bike, in the snow? Is this true, what Henni says?"

"*Arabelle's* bike."

"I don't care whose bike."

"You asked about true. I'm just saying."

"Ada."

"Listen, Mutti. I wasn't looking for trouble. I swear it." I try to catch her eye, want her to believe me, wish that everything in this world didn't make her so afraid of every choice that every single one of us, every single day, is making. But she stares into her Garfield mug, spooning the soup with her delicate fury. She looks into her soup, and not at me. It makes arguing hard, makes me feel sicker.

"Look where you are," she says after a while, trying to keep her voice low, trying to keep this between us, not a fight for the whole co-op. "Look how we live. Trouble finds us." Behind her, on the other side of the window, the snow keeps falling and the dark keeps coming and now Arabelle stands, finds the old book of matches and a new wax stub and puts a flame down into one of Omi's short votives.

"Savas is a little kid, Mutti," I say, as the fire wicks. "And he was scared, and I found him, and what was I supposed to do? What would you have wanted me to do? What would you have done? Leave him be, Mutti? Leave him alone in the church under the rack of coats, shivering away in his PJs?" I don't feel that great, and I'm talking too much. And Mutti won't look up when she should. I wish she'd push her hair out of her face and lift her chin and see me.

"I'm talking about your first choice, Ada. The choice you make, every night, to leave in here for out there. To think nothing bad will happen. This is Kreuzberg. This is now."

"But aren't you glad, Mutti? Aren't you glad for Savas's sake that I'm out at night, that I was there? Don't you . . . ?"

"You're fifteen, Ada," she interrupts, her words gaining speed, and volume, her wanting to keep this argument private not as big now as her wanting me to understand. "And every night you're out there with your color cans, arting up the wall, doing whatever you think you are doing, scheming whatever you're scheming, and they could shoot you, you know. They've shot at others. And then what would I do, Ada? Have you thought about that? What would I do without you?"

"Have *you* thought, Mutti, about you, about where you go? Have *you*?"

"This is not about me."

"It's about us. It's about right now." The words are wide red throbs in the tunnel of my throat. It hurts my tongue to talk, also my ears.

"Both of you," Omi says now. "Quiet. We'll eat in peace." She has been eating. Her soup is gone—every last fold of cabbage and lettuce, every parsley freckle. She gives Arabelle the eye and slides her the pan and Arabelle stands and slowly ladles in, her dreadlocks thickening with the steam and the small rise of her belly showing beneath her striped T-shirt. She's five months forward and Peter doesn't know and if she doesn't tell him soon he'll be gone, back to America, to whatever he's left back there. Man on a Mission, Arabelle calls Peter, my American Romantic, and the clock ticks and she's here, staring down at the city of vegetables through her wire-rimmed glasses, her eyes magnified and focused, her sides not chosen—friend to my mother, friend to me. She slides the saucepan back toward Omi. Mutti puts her face in her hands, keeps the line of silver pink from showing.

"I know Savas's mom," Arabelle says now, leaving the ladle to rest in the pot and sitting back down, fitting her fingers up beneath her lenses and rubbing at the most chocolate-colored parts of her tiredness.

"Excuse me?" I ask, very quietly now.

"I mean," Arabelle says, "I know about her. I know the stories the ladies at the Köpi tell. I know that she's in trouble."

FRIEDRICHSHAIN

★

You learned the number eight by tracing your grandfather's face, which cinched in at his ears but was wide in all other places. You learned the stars from him. You learned waiting. He had round blue eyes, one shelved higher than the other. He had a tooth that turned in at a sharp angle, no hair on his head, a purple vein that ran a river from one ear to one eye.

"You'll be man of the house," he told you. "Until we're together again."

"Say goodbye, Stefan."

"No."

"Look at your grandfather."

You wouldn't.

"You'll be late, Jorge. Leave him be."

"Stefan?"

"No."

But he waited for you. He got down on one knee. He took off his gray felt hat and shined his naked head. He smiled at you beneath his mustache. "I'm going to find her," he said. "I'm going to find her and bring her back."

Then he stood up and you thought he was leaving, you thought this was it, you almost cried, you were crying, but he was going toward the closet instead, turning the knob on the door, pushing his arms between the old bear coats, the nylon raincoats, the wet boots strung by their tied laces. He was in there and you couldn't see anything but the back of his boots and the puddled black of his long wool coat on the floor and your grandmother walking back and forth, pacing, hooking her hands into the buckle on her belt, telling him to hurry. Her hands were shaking, but her voice was clear. She was watching the door, watching him through glasses steamed up with her crying, telling him to hurry, looking at you because it was your fault that he was in there digging. Your fault that he was making himself late. Your fault—everything.

And then he was back there, in front of you, back on his knees. His body folded in half, his figure-eight face near to yours, those blue eyes, each on their own shelf. "This is for you," he said, and it was there, on the wide bent plane above his knees—black and thin, narrow. He had large brown freckles. His face was islands and rivers.

But you closed your fists, pushed out your lip, would not look up at him. He put his fingers to your chin. He said your name. He waited. That is the sin, that is the crime: He waited.

"Look at me, Stefan."

"I won't."

"Look at me."

"I won't. You're leaving."

"Don't be stubborn, Stefan. There isn't time."

"You said . . ."

"Take this," he finally said. "It's yours." Balancing the scope on his knees and opening your fists with his hands and rolling the thing from him to you. You almost fell down from the weight of it, the cold of it, the rattling up of the screws inside, the rack and pinions, the mirror cell, glass. You looked up and you were there, in the blue of his eyes, two versions of you in your birthday haircut and your too-big cardigan.

"The world is in here," he was saying, tapping the scope with one hand. "The world is in here. You find it."

"You'll be late," my grandmother said then, her voice afraid. "It'll go wrong, Jorge. Please." Her big belt buckle was a mean, toothy thing. She wore a dark turtleneck, black slippers.

"There's time."

"There isn't."

"It's all right."

"You promised."

"I still promise," he said, and he was unfolding, standing, getting up off one knee and then off the other, putting the hat back on his naked head, standing there, the great tree of him, the purple river running ear to eye. He kissed her once on either cheek, and then, for a long, quiet time, on her lips. He was so much taller that he had to bend his knees. She was so much shorter that her two feet left the floor.

"Man of the house," he said, looking at you. He said it, and he didn't come back. You waited.

SO36

*

The candle's gone out twice on Arabelle telling the story of Savas's mom, and now the room is dark, but no one moves. There are five of us here, if you count Arabelle's baby. Still, the rooms feel black and empty.

"So she had no choice," Omi says at last.

"No choice," Mutti repeats, her words soft and heartbroken.

More silence rushes in.

FRIEDRICHSHAIN

★

Last night the snow was thick and the signals went dead. There was no one alive but Grossmutter. She sat on the upholstered chair for a long time staring at the empty TV screen, and after you came in from outside, where the snow had climbed up past your knees and numbed your toes and made your lips feel blue, you sat beside her not talking. Grossmutter is not a woman drowned in her tears. She is a woman mummified. What she wants is not here. Who she loves is gone. She sits and she waits for the end of time, but if you leave here—if you were to leave, how could you leave?—she'd have to get out, too. If you leave it has to be clean.

"Just look at it," Ada said, last time she was here. "Look at it and tell me why not."

She was lying beside you on your too-small bed, her head just below your ribs. You had been looking at the maps of stars you had taped up to the ceiling—old maps thin and crease-blurred. You had been explaining, pointing, left to right: Leo,

Cancer, Gemini, Auriga, Taurus, Aries, Pisces. Then Perseus above and Orion below. Then Canis Minor and Ursa Major. It was a winter evening in the northern hemisphere on the paper above your head. You thought she was listening. You stopped. She was quiet, her body curled into you like a seed. You could see the black part of her hair that was growing out and how the part between the black and the pink was gold, and you were touching the gold and now she lifted her head and propped it up with a hand, your bed so skinny that she had to work hard not to fall off.

"When you're free, will you go to find her?" she asked.

It was a dumb question, two impossibles. "No."

"Don't you want to? Aren't you curious?"

"She should be curious about me."

"Maybe she can't be."

"Can't be curious?"

"Maybe she can't, Stefan. You don't know until you know." She was sliding and you caught her. You shifted over in the bed.

"She shouldn't have run in the first place."

"Maybe she couldn't help it."

"Maybe doesn't count, Ada. Not when she's your mother."

"Forgiveness is better than no forgiveness," Ada said after a long time, and then she dropped her head back down to your stomach and stayed like that, not talking, and you didn't want her to be mad because there's no time to be mad, there's no time for anything when you're in love with a West Berliner.

You stared at the star maps and the stars were going nowhere. You listened to the crackle of talk beyond your door, where your two grandmothers were sitting, the radio on, the volume up, the noise masquerading around their words. There's a little one-drawer table beside your bed. You gave the knob a yank; Ada didn't budge. You felt around inside the drawer until you had what you wanted, and then you held it in your hand just so—above your face, so you could read it.

"What are you doing?" Ada asked, after a long time.

"Reading."

"Reading what?"

"Come up here on my pillow. Come up here, and I'll show you."

"I can't."

"Why not?"

"I'm mad."

"Come on." You pulled her toward you, pulled her deliciously near. She turned and was above you and was mad but not too mad to kiss you. Her body's sweet and thin but in the right places round. She smells like cinnamon. You hardly moved but the bed still squealed. You stopped, and it went silent. Again, you kissed her.

"Maybe," you said.

"Maybe what?"

"Maybe maybe matters."

"What, Stefan? Don't tease me." Her lips were puffy with all the kissing, like gum before the pop. She pulled herself up and away, and sat there on your stomach, and suddenly she was little again—the kid who would show up with the pigtails and hide behind her grandmother's legs. The crayon-hoarding kid beneath the table. The questions asked out beneath the stars. The in-your-way kid, like a puppy or a cat. You could see the kid she was then despite the girl she is now—the Cleopatra eyes and the Depeche T-shirt, the splatter of paint on her skin. She's just a girl. She is your girl. You'd do anything for her, almost.

"What?" she asked again, and you felt around on the floor for the thing you'd dropped in the middle of all the kissing, and there it was. The article she'd brought all the way here inside her boots—crumpled and folded and unfolded, more creases than the star maps, more black holes. "The Great Escapes," the story was called, and it had all the details.

"You mean it?" she said. It was like she was trying to see you for you. Measure you up with her eyes. That was November, and now it's February, and when she comes again she will ask for your plan and the thing is, you don't have one. You want her to have faith in you, and if she did, wouldn't you naturally have faith in yourself? At least, just for the day.

"Where would you go," you ask your grandmother now, in the dark, the TV black, "if you could go anywhere?"

"Back," she says without a moment's pause. "I'd go back to then." And she means the night when you were small and your grandfather was leaving. She means she'd make it different. You wouldn't say goodbye. You made your grandfather stop. You made him dig through the closet, bring out his scope, wait for you to accept it. Take all of that away, erase it, and maybe he wouldn't have vanished. Maybe he would have gone, found the way, come back, and saved you—taken you with him to freedom. Maybe he would have met his friends at the pub at the right hour. Maybe he would have gone safe, to the tunnel. Crawled through first, maybe, or third, but not last and not alone—not after the tunnel beneath the streets, beneath the fenced-up border line, had already begun fracturing, collapsing. The water seeping in from a sewer above and fingering its way through the sand and between the reinforcements and scurrying down and through until it reached a soft, dirty spot. The walls gave up, that's what happened. And some of the East Berliners made it through, most of them did, but not your grandfather. Your grandfather vanished. No body. No proof. But he's gone.

You made him late, and your grandmother will never forgive you, and the truth is: You never will forgive yourself.

Forgiveness is better than no forgiveness, Ada says. But there are things you haven't told her. Things you can't explain.

SO36

*

We hear Arabelle's boots clomp the hall outside, then down
the stairs and out and into the slush of the snow and through
the first courtyard, under the arch, over the buried steel tracks,
toward her own corner of this commune. Timur's basil box
will be snuffed out by now. Arabelle's bike will be slicked and
frozen. Gretchen and her lover will be asleep, the dealers, too,
and the other tattoo artists, and the two old ladies who walk
Kreuzberg hand-in-hand, everywhere they go it's hand-in-hand,
and Gunter who is still in love with Marlene Dietrich and will
never stop loving Marlene Dietrich, and the bead-stringers in
the corner shop. Everyone's asleep, or everyone's watching the
snow. Mutti has gone to her room and closed the door. Omi
has ladled the last of the *Eintopf* into her saucepan and is stirring very slow, the spoon banging shyly against the inside metal
making a dull song. She brings the last of the carrots to her lips
and closes her eyes like it's the first taste of anything all evening.

"It's good, isn't it?" she asks, after she swallows.

I nod. The candle's gone out. There is wind beyond the windows, and beyond the windows are Savas and his mother, and they need us. She had been planning to leave, Arabelle said, when her husband found out. She had asked the women of the Köpi for their help, and with the marks they'd earned from the sweaters they'd knit, with the pfennigs they hid in their long coat pockets, they had raised enough for two tickets home. Savas's mother was twenty years old and two days away from gone. This is what Arabelle said, the story Savas's aunt had told in the workshop with the women with their curlicue accents. They unwrap their heads and their hair falls forward and their knitting needles click and Arabelle teaches them German and they talk—whatever words they can find are their stories. A few days ago, Arabelle said, they were talking about a boy named Savas and worrying about his mother, who had been beaten again, the bone beneath her one eye shattered, and she was going home. Packing her bags and taking Savas back to the Anatolian farmlands of Turkey and her own red flag and language, leaving the man she had been promised to and would not ever love. She was leaving, but her plans had been found out, and the women of the Köpi had talked of this, had asked for words, and Arabelle had walked among them as their needles clicked—listening and teaching, taking account.

"You're worrying about Savas," Omi says now, the saucepan gone dry, the whole world silent.

I stare at her through the dark, a level stare. "I should have stopped her," I say. "I should have helped."

"Nothing to do," she says.

"Why not?"

"Because people who run don't want to be caught. People who hide don't want to be found." She dabs at her chin with her thumb, a bristling sound. She dares me to contradict her, but there's no point to it. I know what happened at the end of the war, when the Germans had lost and the Russians moved in, and when Omi, more than anything else, did not want to be found.

"Savas is afraid," I say.

"We don't need more trouble here," she says. "We have enough."

The air is cold. The room is dark. I will write to Stefan tomorrow.

*

Beneath the quilt on the couch the fever heat runs between my breasts and pools—a hot trickle. I yank at the quilt and the air ices through me. I snatch the quilt back to my chin and the fever runs. The cold is in my bones and the heat is in my skin. I'm between sleeping and dreaming, lost in Berlin.

Sometime, late, I wake to the sound of Omi snoring behind the door to her room. She takes a long, rasping time filling her lungs, then snorts the air out quick, and then it's silence, then rumbling again. Who knows how she sleeps. *People who hide don't want to be found,* she said, and now when I close my eyes it's her world, the stories she's told me. The Red Army has made its way in, is crossing the river. There are German traitors— deserters—strung up by their flimsy necks from the lampposts at train stations, and women and children are almost all that is left of Berlin. There will be no virgins standing after everything is done, and the newspapers have stopped, and the phones ring empty, and the trains run two to three to a car while everybody else walks, because no one else, including Omi, can afford the fare; they have all been issued the wrong ration cards. She will wait in many lines. She will fight for rancid butter. She will loot the abandoned bakery for whatever there still is, and at night she will warm her feet by that brick, her legs cold and white beside her mother's. When the bombs go off she will scramble, her heart high and sick in her throat. She will run, buckets of stolen things in each hand, the buckets clanging. She will run beneath the streets into the shelter.

Omi is hiding. The shelter is dark, but Omi will be found, and her mother, and her best friend, Katja, too, who can trade cigarettes for flour, a used pair of boots for a wool jacket, a tulip bulb for a bird in a cage, and who will grow up and be old, who will become Stefan's Grossmutter.

People who hide don't want to be found. But Savas is out there, running. All night long, I crack and sweat, and all night long, he's running, and what I need is a boy named Stefan. I need Stefan to help me. I feel my way to the kitchen and the book of matches. I strike a light, touch it to the wick. I tear a page from my journal of sketches and write the single word I'll mail tomorrow:

Now.

✱

I wake to Mutti's hand on my head, her eyes big in the powdered morning light.

"You were talking in your sleep again."

"Didn't mean it."

She turns her hand the other way, touches my forehead with her knuckles. "So many stories," she says. She waits. Closes her eyes. Her forehead wrinkles. "Fever's gone."

I shrug my shoulders and they don't hurt. I bring my knees up toward my chin, or as far as I can before Mutti's weight on the quilt tugs me down. I wonder how long she's been sitting here, listening to my babble. "I was dreaming about Savas."

"Savas is a Turkish boy, Ada."

I give her a funny look.

"You kept saying the Russians were coming."

I wriggle my arms free of the quilt, push my hair out of my face, try to think myself backward into my dreams, remember what I said out loud that brought Mutti here, beside me. I listen for the sound of sleep behind Omi's door, look for the page that I'd torn from my book. I hear it crackle beneath my pillow.

"What are you going to do?" Mutti asks.

"About what?"

"I know you, Ada. You're scheming."

There are hard lines beneath my mother's eyes and shadows caught between them. Her hair is thistles. The light from the window glows through it, then storms her face with a sea-colored green. Sometimes when I look at my mother's face I see every man she ever loved and how much loving bruised her.

"I think it's pretty obvious."

"What is?"

"That there's nothing I can do."

"Nothing?"

"It's impossible, Mutti. You know how it is. The Turks are their own country. I can't save Savas." I won't talk about Stefan, because the worry will kill her. She'll tell Omi and Omi will tell Stefan's Grossmutter, and every shot I have at happiness will be gone.

Mutti straightens then shivers with the cold, unsatisfied. She pulls her thin sweater across her chest and buttons it up to her chin, knows that I'm lying in multiple dimensions, knows that if I knew how to rescue Savas I would. If I knew where to find him, that's where I'd be. If I knew Stefan would come, I'd open the door.

She stares at me for a long time. Draws her index finger across the bridge of my nose. "Impossible has never stopped you," she says, and I wonder how much she knows about everything I'll always want. I wonder whether, in my dreams, I called out for Stefan.

"You can't save the world, Ada. You know that, don't you?"

"Somebody has to try," I say, and I see the hurt go through her.

FRIEDRICHSHAIN

★

Outside the snow keeps falling—so thick now that soon the buses will stop and the only way around will be by foot, straight up to your knees in the white. Everything is silent. Everything is white. You're thinking about Heinz Holzapfel again, and how he got free on his own.

"Read it," Ada had said, when she was here, and you told her you would and she wouldn't believe you, but the truth is you've read Holzapfel's story every night since the last time she kissed you. You have read it and creased it and uncreased it, whitened the words with your thumb, slipped it back into that tuck of space between your mattress and your bed frame, then pulled it back into the light again, where it smells of the inside of Ada's boot.

"Do you think your grandmother even loves you?" Ada asked.

"I don't know," you said. Because you don't.

SWOOPS ACROSS WALL:
FAMILY MAKES DARING ESCAPE

Berlin (AP)—In one of the boldest escapes of the cold war, an East German economist, his wife and their 9-year-old son swung themselves in a homemade cable harness from the roof of a heavily guarded Communist government building to the safety of West Berlin.

They came down over the barbed wire–topped wall Wednesday night from the top of the five-story "House of Ministries" where East German Premier Willi Stoph has offices.

"I was 80 percent certain that the plan would succeed, because everything had been well prepared and besides I had helpers in West Berlin.

"Often I had occasion to visit the Ministries building on business but in the building itself I had no help."

Holzapfel took his family into the building Wednesday and at 5 P.M. they went into an attic room, where they stayed until 10 P.M.

The boy slept most of the time, and when it was time to get ready the father woke him with these words, "Now we are going to uncle. There you will get the bicycle we promised you. But first you must show your courage, because until now you have earned only the [bicycle's] turn signal and bell."

The boy remained quiet and "we went out of the room onto the roof. It was pouring rain. We wanted to be across by 11 P.M., but it took much more time."

Holzapfel had a nylon-type cord about as thick as a tennis racket string tied to a hammer. His preparations were thorough. He had painted the hammer handle with phosphorous so that those waiting in West Berlin would see it when he threw it. So that it would make no noise when it landed, he had padded the hammer head.

Those in the West fastened a heavy cable to the hammer and Heinz and Jutta pulled it to them, "taking all our strength."

"Now we were ready to begin the most dangerous part of our flight."

"We were all very quiet. Guenter was sent over first."

Holzapfel explained he had made a pulley out of a bicycle wheel axle, with a shoulder and waist harness slung underneath. They hung on to an attachment and rolled down the cable.

"You see how easy it is," Ada had said, when she was here the last time. Her weight in your arms. Her smell in your nose. Her hair tickling the soft parts of your neck, where the stubble still doesn't grow. "Just a few parts and some string," she said. "Just a wheel and a harness."

"There's nothing easy about it," you said, and she said, "Like there's anything easy about this." Meaning her and us. Meaning stuck in time. But leaving is permanent, and failure lasts.

"Stefan," Grossmutter calls, and you hear the shuffle of her slippered feet toward you.

"Yes?"

"You'll be late for the Eisfabrik," she says. And studies you with the pinch of her eyes.

SO36

*

I'm wearing black patent-leather boots with a zipper up each calf, gray cabled tights, a corduroy jumper, and a long leather coat I borrowed from Gretchen, who stopped by early with a bowl of oatmeal and molasses; news travels fast when you're squatters. There's cold in my eyes and winter in my lungs, and when I call for Savas his name scorches through me.

Near the Landwehrkanal the vendor trucks are rutting the snow with their wide wheels, leaving grooves shellacked by the morning sun. Little girls in pink hats and boys with red mittens run the grooves—building speed with quick sprints then boot-tobogganing through. From behind, the mothers nag and warn, their heads wrapped twice in scarves, their jilbabs long over their stockinged feet and winter sandals. The smell is snow and sun but also pumpkin seeds and coffee, *gözleme* and boiled corn, used batteries and leather. I walk Oranienstrasse toward Heinrichplatz. I walk past buildings that are white, pink, yellow, old with bullet holes, beneath windows where spatulas scrape against pans. Iced sheets are being unclipped from lines above. Someone is crying, but it isn't Savas. The chill is back in my bones. School starts in an hour and I'll be late again. I've mailed the letter I wrote.

"Where do you think you're going?" Omi asked before I left.

"I have to find him," I said.

"What did I tell you?" she said, and her eyes were small as I closed the door.

Savas's hair is black and in the sun it's almost blue. There's a pinch in his brow when he thinks. There's a way he has of holding your hand—like he's the one in charge, like he's protecting. There are other women, Arabelle says, who have tried to leave and who have been found dead later, murdered by husbands angry at them for removing their burqas or looking for a job or hoping to speak German in Germany. There are kids who get lost and no one finds them. I think of Arabelle at the shop with the Turkish women, trading their language for German, their submission for power. I think of Peter, Arabelle's lover, who says the Turks will not learn to save themselves until the Germans give them protection—give them papers and give them rights, give them police, when they need it. He gives them German words for what has been taken, pounds in about landlords, bosses, teachers, lectures in coffee shops and crowded salons, on street corners and in mosques, sits with the men of the Black Sea and plays their card games and tells them how to make it happen. Workers' unions. Workers' rights. You Turks are not outsiders or *Gastarbeiter*, he tells them. You Turks are not the ghetto. You are the people crowded into lousy housing and paid less than you are worth and tossed to the gutter when your hips give in and your bones shatter and the black factory air you breathe stays permanent in your lungs. You are human beings, Peter tells them. Organize, he insists. Keep yourselves and those among you safe.

Take what you are owed.

Command respect.

Peter's hair is red fire and his glasses are John Lennon. His skin is so American pale that you can see his thoughts flick through it, and it worries Arabelle, how he's made himself dangerous with his own agitations, how he signs his name to the proclamations he glues to lampposts and to walls, how he lets nothing get in the way of his idealism. I don't know what will happen, Arabelle says, because Peter's time in Germany is almost up; his visa's running short. He'll return to the States and to graduate school, finish his thesis, send postcards, unless. And of course we both know what *unless* means. Unless there's a wedding in Kreuzberg.

"Tell him about the baby," I say.

"He has to love me," she says, "for the right reasons."

"Savas," I call. "Savas!" And the cold is straight through to my toes and knees, and my head is still weird from the fever, and when I call again my voice goes short—a word at the end of a wire. The kids tobogganing the grooves are still running, waving their mittened hands like United Nations flags, but none of them are Savas. None are the little boy from St. Thomas Day Care who sits in my lap when I read about fear or holds my hand when I'm missing Stefan or tips down slightly when he says my name, as if I were an actual princess.

People who hide don't want to be found, Omi says. But Savas is just a little boy, and maybe hiding is not what Savas wants, and maybe what happens next will be my fault: I shouldn't have let him vanish. And maybe, also, I should confess to this: Mailing a word like *now* across the border wasn't exactly Stasi smart.

*

"Just walking around," Henni says now, arching the pencil line of her left eyebrow and smudging the fringes of her lashes with an incredulous finger. "Looking?"

"Yeah," I say, feeling stupid. "Looking for Savas."

On the other side of the kitchen wall, the kids are playing a game of Pied Piper, Markus in the lead being his skinny, tall self. Through the cutout window above the sink I watch him prancing in his green felt cap. The kids swarm Markus, forgetting their places in the line. They toot through their fingers and their plastic zurnas, Brigitte sucking her three fingers and Aylin wearing a paper crown. They finished their puppets and put on their show when I was gone. They made finger paintings that hang now, dry, from the clothesline that shimmies over their heads in the room. The church bells ring the eleven o'clock hour, but Markus keeps prancing and the kids keep following, all except Meryem, who stands at the window looking out onto the snow that's been flattened, browned, and yellowed.

Through the bank of windows along the exterior wall the sun throws down a white line. Henni stands with her clogs toeing up to one side and I stand in the socks she pulled out of the dryer, some fuzzy lost-and-founds, one of them lime green and the other olive-colored. Deep inside I'm starting to thaw. My knees and my ankles feel crunchy. We watch the kids through the cutout window. Chaos could hit at any second.

"Did you really think he'd just appear, Ada? That walking for hours in the cold after you've been home sick for days was the best use of your time?"

"Sorry, Henni."

"You've missed several days of work after a lot of coming in late, you get your mother and your grandmother so worried they come out to find me, to ask me questions, to see where you've been, what you've been saying—in a blizzard, no less, Ada—and the first thing you do when you're well enough is go walking around in Little Istanbul thinking maybe, just maybe, you'll see Savas."

"The *Eintopf* was really good, by the way."

"Don't change the subject."

I bite the speckled cuticles of my little pinky. "I didn't have a better plan."

Henni throws both arms up, flabby and unhappy, like it's just one more stupid thing I've said.

"Arabelle says—"

"Who's Arabelle?"

"The one with the bike."

Henni's eyes track side to side, back and forth, trying to remember. Out behind Markus the kids are spinning and hiding, yelping and giggling, and if they don't back down soon the minister will open the door to his office and walk down the hall and step in among us, ask if everything's fine. He'll rub at the bald place beneath his hair and shake his head like he still can't decide whether having a multicultural day care in an empty room in his administrative wing is the smartest thing for St. Thomas.

"Go on," Henni tells me.

"Shouldn't we help Markus?" I say, because I don't know how to go on, because I want to, but I can't.

"Finish your story."

I try to think of where to start. I feel a little clutch in my heart. "Arabelle says Savas's mother is in really big trouble," I start. "She says people like her can die in Little Istanbul and nobody will know and their children could die, too. I don't know how to find them, do you? I don't know what to do. But, Henni: It's Savas."

The Pied Piper's still marching, but the kids have lost the song. They're jumping on the table now, hiding under the chairs, chasing each other into the closet, all except for Meryem, who has climbed up onto the windowsill. I watch the kids through the interior window; Henni does, too. My job is out there with them. My knees are still crunchy. I look ridiculous in these lost-and-found socks, my legs so bare, my cabled tights spinning in the dryer. I look ridiculous, and Savas is missing. He should be out there with the others, leader of the band.

"And Arabelle knows this because . . . ?" Henni asks now, her voice measured and her blue eyes bright on me.

"Because of her job. She works at the Köpi, the co-op where the Turkish ladies knit."

Henni blinks twice. Pauses. "This is your friend with the bike."

"Yes."

"What kind of trouble does she say Savas is in?" she finally asks, her eyes steady on me, the fat fringes of her lashes smudged. In the big room the twins are banging on the table. Brigitte has glue in her hair. Any second, I think, and the day care will explode. The minister will show his head. Someone will be planning to come and shut us down.

"Savas's mom was forced to marry Savas's dad," I say, repeating what Arabelle told me. "She was sent here from Anatolia—put on a plane six years ago, married to this guy she'd never met. Second cousin or something. He's forty-one and she's twenty, and he beats her whenever he wants to, broke a bone in her face, Henni. She's had enough of it, you know, and she's trying to get back home—back to Turkey where her mother is, back to the farms she came from. She's trying to get home and the Köpi ladies were helping, raising money for her tickets, making arrangements. But the sicko-husband found her suitcase and he beat her. He locked her in a room and by the time she got out, all her clothes were gone, all her papers, her passport, the money that the ladies raised, her tickets. When she started to cry he hit her worse, and Savas was there. Savas was watching. That's why he ran away. That's what Arabelle says. That's what the Köpi ladies told her. One of them saw Savas leave. Another heard his mother running. None of them know where they've gone."

Henni takes in a big long breath, and I do, too. We stand there in the kitchen, watching each other—Henni looking for signs of truth from me, me looking for a real plan from her.

"Bastard," she says at last.

"Yeah," I say.

"And Savas saw all this?"

"*Love is a bad thing.* That's what he told me, Henni."

Henni bites the inside of her cheek and closes her eyes. She gets a million lines of worry in her forehead. I can see her playing the story through, trying to imagine, but stuck. In the room beyond us, Ece's crying, both fists up to her eyes. Aylin's lost her crown and she can't find it. Markus has stopped the Pied Piper parade. Meryem is still turned away from it all, her little body perched up on the windowsill, her red shoes dangling out over the edge. She's got something in her hand, I see, and when I squint I realize what it is: Savas's playdough dragon.

"So we should call the police," I say. "We should do something."

"You know how it is. They won't get involved. They need hard evidence—a lot of it—before they'll get involved with a domestic dispute among the Turks."

"It's not just some *dispute,* Henni."

"What proof do we have? Think about it."

"Savas isn't here," I say. "Isn't that evidence enough?"

"This is a day care, Ada. Kids come and go."

"But Savas ran here. By himself. At night."

"And you're the only one who saw him, Ada. It's not enough to save a Turk in Kreuzberg."

"There are the Köpi ladies. Arabelle's friends. Maybe—"

"Think about it, Ada. If they talk to the German police they'll be in trouble at home. They are learning German as a secret, remember? Their husbands haven't been told."

"So what's our plan?" I hear my voice and it's pleading— too loud and so high that some of the kids in the classroom turn and watch us through the interior window, which is wide and short, its frame painted yellow on one side and left bare and knotted pine on the other.

"I don't know," Henni says. "I'm thinking on it."

*

The kids are all settled onto the storytelling rug by the time I go in to greet them—Markus made it happen, so I thank him. They watch me, different than before, like I'm a stranger to them, like being gone for a few days means I forgot them. Forgot how one twin sits perfectly still and the other one fidgets. Forgot the high shrug of Brigitte's shoulders. Forgot who sucks which fingers and who calls out and who has to be invited, every time, to say what she is thinking. I prop myself up on the too-small chair and wrestle the big book up onto my lap. I tell them that they have to come closer to hear, and one by one, on elbows and knees, they scoot forward—the paint in their fingernails, the smell of their playdough, the stain of their juice, the smashed dust bunnies on their sock toes.

"Meryem," I say, "do you want to come and join us?" Because she hasn't moved from the window ledge and she's holding Savas's dragon like an old-world talisman.

"No thank you, Miss Ada," she says.

"Are you sure, Meryem?" Normally I would press but today I don't. Today Meryem is watching the window, looking out, I sense, for all of us. She has her reasons and the other kids don't mind. They let her be, her back to us, her one ear cocked in our direction.

I turn the big cardboard pages slow—past the thieves in the den, past the dead in the cemetery, past the lonely house and the storm at sea.

"Where is the fear?" I ask the kids, and at every picture they shake their heads no. It's not here or here or here or here. The boy can't find his fear. We come to the page where we'd stopped the last time.

"What's going to happen?" I ask, my voice in a hush.

"Fear's coming," Meryem says, from her perch on the ledge. "Fear's coming, Miss Ada. I know it."

I turn around and she's facing forward. Her eyes are big black lakes, wind-rippled. She clutches the dragon close and reaches one arm for me. I lay the book on the floor and stand to catch her. She wraps her arm around my neck and her legs around my waist. Her skin is warm and clammy. "Hey," I say, but she just clings harder, and now when I sit us both down onto the tiny chair, I feel its silver legs tremble.

"I think it's juice time," I say, but the kids don't move. They stay where they were—quiet, frozen. Finally Daniel raises his hand. "Miss Ada," he says, "Savas is missing."

"I know," I say. "We're looking for him."

"Where's Savas?" Aysel says, twisting her arms up and locking her fingers, rocking back and forth now, and now Daniel's rocking, too, and even Aylin starts moving—an agitation, a fever.

And now Meryem starts crying. Henni appears in an instant, like Henni does, calling the kids to the table for juice. They don't really know what they want to do. They sit there watching each other, looking at me, looking at the table, looking at Henni with her bright red plastic pitcher. One by one, they wrestle themselves up from the floor and onto their stockinged toes and make their way to the table.

"Meryem," I say, but her grip is growing tighter. "Do you want some juice, sweetheart?"

But her tears trickle down her cheek, onto my neck. They pool above my heart—hot and clotted. "Savas is afraid," she says, and that's all she'll say, the rest of this whole day, until her mother comes to get her.

"We need to find him," I say to Henni before I leave—when it's just us again, no kids, no Markus. When we've talked it through all over again—the phone that keeps ringing, the father who won't want us, the mother who has vanished.

"I'm working on a plan," she says. "Go home, okay? Come back tomorrow. We're going to do what we can."

FRIEDRICHSHAIN

★

In the apartment, Grossmutter plays the TV so loud the neighbors knock at the walls, hit the floor with the stick of a broom: *Turn it down.* She acts like she can't hear the complaints, can't feel the floor shaking, doesn't know the walls are rattling, the Lenins and Stalins in their picture frames, the photos of you, the former Pioneer. Only when the girl across the hall knocks and says *please,* offers a glass of cold milk for her troubles, does your Grossmutter snap the TV off, and then she sits in the dark and the silence. Days go by, darkened and silent until one afternoon, late, the sun banked in low with the pan-bottom clouds, she finds you on the balcony and asks to see. She's wearing her housecoat under her overcoat and her embroidered slippers. She's wearing sandbags beneath both of her eyes. She's short, and you adjust your machine. She's quiet, and you don't know what she needs. When you tip the scope up, toward where the stars are supposed to be, she shakes her head no, definitely not.

There's a place out there—a building, a room. She adjusts and she fiddles but she can't find it. Her mouth works itself into a fever. She claws at the bags beneath her eyes, tries again, exhaling the cold smoke of the weather.

"That's the one," she says, finally, moving her head away so you can see. The view comes in big and distorted. It's an old three-story building on a crooked street. "There was a movie theater," she says, "to the left of it. There was a baker down on the corner. It was somebody's house, somebody's parlor. That was the West, and that was then."

"Grossmutter?"

"When I think of how we survived," she says. "And where." Her words are soft. Her fingers are on her lips. She goes inside, turns the TV on, comes back out, rubbing those sandbags. The old miser in the apartment below starts knocking the floor with his broomstick. *Turn it down.* She doesn't. She needs the noise to tell me a story. The ankles above her slippers are turning bruise-blue with the cold.

"We were young," she says, whispering beneath the newscaster's baritone. "We protected each other."

You don't ask, because you know more's coming. Because you know that all this time, all these late afternoons and nights while you've been sketching, scheming, planning, she's been working on telling you something true.

"I was one year older than you," she says. "And my best friend was having a baby."

She gets tears in her eyes. She looks a thousand years old. She is so tiny.

"We had to *do* things," she says. "We had to *survive,* you understand?"

"It was the war," you say.

"We were young," she says. "And the worst was still to come. Divisions," she says. "Heartbreaks. That goddamned crucifying wall." She shudders, but there's no keeping out the cold, no rolling back the clock to August 13, 1961, *Stacheldrahtsonntag,* Barbed-Wire Sunday. You've been told the story so many times it's like you were there yourself, waking up inside the coil of a cage. Barbed wire like deadly bales between apartment houses. Barbed wire across the S-Bahn. Barbed wire slashing phone lines, sewers, friends, marriages, and families. By sealing the West German border, Comrade Erich Honecker had imprisoned East Berlin. He'd put in the trace of a first wall, and now the wall is what the wall has become—concrete and watchtowers, asparagus grass and dogs, trip flares and tank traps. Grossmutter has lived it all. You have lived a too-long fraction. Her heartbreaks aren't your heartbreaks, but she knows what aching is. She knows what it would mean to be free.

She yanks both coats across her chest, still feels the cold. She protects herself, and you can't help her, and this, you think, is what she means to say. That surviving has its costs. That only and merely surviving has its costs, too.

"Look," you say, "the city's gone dark." Because all of a sudden it has—the round lights in the smirking windows, the bit of reflection across the canal, the sharp electric needle of the Fernsehturm. You search the low horizon for a flash of pink.

"Something's come for you, Stefan," she says, a whisper.

An envelope in her pocket.

SO36

*

Arabelle's waiting for me in the courtyard's dark—her breath frosty white, her arms folded tight over the long knitted coat that strains at her belly. Her eyes are catching the light of the first-floor TVs. She's tied the ropes of her hair into a ponytail and wears her glasses high on her forehead, aviator style. Her gloves are bright pink, fresh from the Köpi. There's a pack of tissues tipping out of one coat pocket, a pair of canvas sneakers on her feet, already splattered with something. She inhales and exhales and the courtyard breathes with her. She opens her mouth and smiles, swings one wide-thighed leg over the seat of her bike, and it's clear: That machine is going nowhere without her.

I give her a long, righteous look, as if the bike were mine in the first place. "Did Mutti put you up to this?" I ask.

"Maybe she thinks you could use some company," Arabelle says.

"I work alone at night," I say.

"Most of the time, yeah. But not tonight." She doesn't budge. She just half sits, half stands there, a patch of the late-night news playing at an angle off her glasses.

"Come on, Arabelle."

"You're not winning this one, all right? You've been sick and you've been acting crazy. Mutti wants you safe, and so I promised."

She turns and slides her butt back on the banana seat to make room for me up front, rubbing my part of the seat with the palm of one hand as if all that plastic sparkle is a magic lantern. I think of walking to my stretch of the wall, hauling my courier bag and cans of paint and lights the whole cold darkened distance. I think of leaving Arabelle here in the courtyard with her woolly-streamered bike and her glow-bright gloves, where she can choose Mutti's side all she wants, if that's how she wants to play it. My best friend acting on behalf of my sad-soaked mother.

"Going or staying?" Arabelle presses.

"Thinking about it."

"Because we can always stay in."

"I've got things to do."

"Then take me with you."

"It's cold out there," I say. "Colder than in here."

"I'm ready for it."

"It's dark and you'll get bored."

"No more excuses. We're going."

"If I wanted a bodyguard, I would have asked you."

"You can pretend I'm not here," she says, "if you want to."

I give her a blast of sour eyeballs. I sigh and the air goes crystal. I strap my bag across my chest and take my place on whatever's left of Arabelle's banana-seat bike. She locks her arms around my waist, fits her chin onto my left shoulder, and one foot to the ground, Flintstones style, I get the bike rolling forward. "I promised your mother you wouldn't go to Kottbusser Tor alone at night," she says, as if the conspiracy she's in on is of our own making. "But that doesn't mean that we're giving up on Savas."

"I wasn't going to the Kottbusser Tor," I say. "Not tonight." I don't have a plan yet. There *is* no plan. No plan for Savas and no word from Stefan. I am worried. I am angry. I feel hot still, and wet, from Meryem's crying. I feel nervous: What does the little girl know? What can't she tell us? Shouldn't I have known how to ask, somehow? Isn't there a better way to listen? Am I just going to keep on messing up like this, letting the kids' confessions pass by me? Letting a boyfriend stay silent?

"Well, then we're good, right? We're good? Mutti won't have to worry."

"She always worries," I say, not turning because I'm steering, avoiding the old metal tracks from the courtyard's factory days and brushing past the piles of snow that Timur shoveled earlier in the day. Timur is what passes for maintenance at our complex. He takes it on himself to keep the basics functioning and the basil growing and everybody else pays him in kind—whatever we have, whatever's left over. That's how it works among squatters at a co-op.

"Mutti worries because Mutti's a mother," Arabelle is saying.

"Are *you* going to be like that when *you're* a mother?" I grunt. It feels like I'm pedaling an extra two tons, like Arabelle's baby is a whole third person.

"I'm already a mother," Arabelle says. "Or haven't you noticed?"

"I'm noticing, Arabelle. Believe me, I am."

There are four years between me and Arabelle. Four years and a million things, but end of the day she's still my best friend and I never can stay mad at her, even when she's earned it. The snow that melted during the day has slicked. The piles of snow that Timur shoveled to each side are dirty white walls, zigging and crusted. I ride a crooked path across the cobblestones and out of the gates onto the street and turn. St. Thomas Church shines in the distance. There's mush and ice and cars and music coming from the bar down the alley. Beneath the wide wheels of Arabelle's bike the ice snaps and the mush goes squish and when a gray cat scampers out from behind a parked truck and I swerve, the belt of Arabelle's arms around me tightens. I'm yanked back and my boot slips. The front wheel wobbles. I get us going again and look up and back at our complex, and there she is, Mutti in the window, her face in a halo of frosted glass.

The branches of the trees along the Mariannenplatz are vanilla frosted. The lights from the old hospital are on and the artists are inside, up on the scaffolding, climbing the ladders, rigging up for a new exhibition. It's always like this on the nights before the shows—like staring into a snow globe and wondering which artist my mother will be falling for next, which ones she already fell for. It's only the artists Mutti loves, never anyone else, and the best artists of all of Kreuzberg are here, at the old hospital which isn't a hospital anymore but one more abandoned space taken over by punkers and painters.

"You think Sebastien's in there?" I ask Arabelle as we push by.

"I don't know," Arabelle says, her words coming out in soft puffs, like she's the one doing the pedaling. "Maybe he is."

We creak and we wobble. We roll past the old hospital toward the front lawn of St. Thomas, which used to be the back lawn of St. Thomas before the wall went up and cut the church off from most of the people it was serving. I watch the dark places and the snowy places, looking for signs of little feet, or for the heat of an open day care window. Nothing. Savas is not out tonight. He has not come back to find me. Above our heads a big bird flies, and then another, escaping the bell tower, and for a split instant I think I see Meryem, hiding in the shadows.

Behind me Arabelle is quiet, her arms still tight. She fits her chin onto my right shoulder and searches the church grounds, too, her glasses still up high on her forehead. We round the church's stone face and head for the narrow space between

St. Thomas and the wall, wobbling a little but keeping our balance. There's only the creaking of the wheels and the knocking of the paint cans, the whisk of the air through the wool streamers, the squeak of the three of us on the blue banana seat that sparkles even at night.

"Almost there," I say, and she says, "I'm ready," and I think of all the times she has asked me about my graffing and all the times I told her to wait, to give me room to finish. Because maybe there are some artists who like to show off midwork, who like to splatter and dab inside the warm space of a snow globe, but I'm not one of those. A work of art has to speak for itself, and it can only speak when it is finished, and besides, my wall is Stefan's wall. I was hoping to show it to him first.

✱

I brake the bike, hop off, steady it for Arabelle, who toes
around on the walk for ice before she trusts both canvas shoes
to the ground. In the thick dark I walk the bike to the base of
the church and prop it up against the wall. When I turn back
around I see Arabelle rubbing the cement slabs with her pink-
mittened fingers as if I'd graffed everything in Braille.

"You going crazy on me again?" I ask.

"No crazier than you out here in the night."

"You can't see anything," I say, "if you stand that close."

"I can't see anything anyway," she says, backing off and
coming toward me.

I unstrap my bag, rattle my cans around, dig until I have
my lights. I switch them on, the first and the second, then balance them both on the bricked-in ledges. It's two sprays of
bright slamming up against my graffing. It's the pictures I've
made, one after the other. The Great Escapes in the order of my
delivery. My butanes and my propanes. My *Ta Da* tag. Arabelle

returns to the wall, removes one mitten, traces the big boot of the running soldier with a finger. She stands back to get a better look at the loaf of bread and the toilet. Back and forth she goes, getting the big picture and the details. The ropes of her hair have fallen loose at her face.

"Ada," she says at last. "Well, Jesus Christ, Ada. You're brilliant with a spray can."

"I'm not finished yet," I say, managing defensiveness and pride at the same time. I feel heat in my face, get down to my business, start pulling my cans out of the bag, my caps, my fingerless gloves, my green bandana. I arrange my colors, dark to light, switch around the caps. It's cold out here. My fingers feel knotty. Arabelle keeps talking.

"You don't have to be finished for me to see," she's saying. "Nobody graffs likes this. Nobody. It's like, you know, Michelangelo quality. I mean, if Michelangelo had a spray can, Ada, Michelangelo would graff like that." Her voice is rising, high on itself. She goes back to the wall, takes her other mitten off, walks the tightrope with her fingers, back and forth, like it's a real, sustaining line. She starts laughing all of a sudden and I have to cut her off.

"Shhh," I say. "The guards will hear you."

She spins quick, like she thinks a uniform with a gun has shown up here beside me. I point to the wall and the places beyond it, where the dogs are sleeping and the guards are on their watch, where the metal spikes of asparagus grass grow underground. In the silence now we hear the rabbits scramble, their bodies too quick and light-boned to be detected by the no-man's-zone land mines that would blast a human into pieces. It's tricked up so good on that side.

"So what are we graffing tonight?" she whispers at last.

"We?"

"I'm out here, aren't I? Put me to work."

"You're out here spying is what you're doing."

"I'm out here as your protectorate."

"My *protectorate*?"

"Whatever. Come on. Don't be such a nudge."

"What do you know about writing, Arabelle?"

"I know everything you're going to teach me." She smiles her full-wattage smile. When I don't smile back she changes her tune. "If I don't do something I'll freeze out here. There's got to be something."

"All right," I say, considering. "You can fill."

"Cool," she says. "How do I fill?"

"Christ," I say. "How can you live in Kreuzberg and not know how to fill?"

"I do other things," she says. "Remember?"

"Yeah. Like spy on your best friend."

I take a can of sky blue and shake it well. I take a can of candy pink and tell her to shake it like I am. The agitator balls go from stuck to rattling free. When the propellant is loose and juiced inside, I tell Arabelle we're ready.

"Some tips," I say, matter-of-fact, showing her how to fit her finger over the valve cap. "We're filling, so we're staying close, all right? Top to bottom with a third overlap and never a continuous press. We're going for a fade fill—blue sky with some sunrise pink. A wall like this sucks the paint right up, so we'll need two coats, maybe three."

"You should teach this stuff."

"I'm already a teacher."

"Yeah, but I mean—"

"You're stalling, Arabelle. I can tell you are."

"Am not."

"Then how about you get started. You keep your wrist moving, okay, but your arm and elbow quiet."

"All right."

"Wait." I crouch back down over the bag, pull two bandanas out. One for her and one for the baby she's carrying. She stoops a little so I can tie the first and then the second. Then I cover my own mouth, and we are ready.

"We look like bandits out here," Arabelle says, her words muffled.

"Have to work quick," I say. "Have to work easy."

She steps back and I show her technique. She steps forward, fits her finger on the valve, and presses down. Color hits the wall and splatters overhead, like one of Stefan's stars exploding. She stands back and I show her again. She moves the can in her hand, changes the angle of her wrist, lifts her elbow up, like she is dancing. Her color makes an even showing. She lifts her finger, laughs.

"What are we filling for?" she asks, after a while.

"Story of a man," I say, "named Holzapfel." I work beside her, a strip of vertical fills. She covers by thirds, working the long horizontals. There's a rhythm to graffing, and she's finding the beat, the loosened strands of her hair falling and rising like the streamers on her bike catching a breeze.

"Who's Holzapfel?" she finally asks.

"A great escapee. The one with the flying fox."

"Oh, God. What's a flying fox?"

"Wheels on a wire," I say, and then I explain. I tell her the story of the night and its rain, of how Heinz Holzapfel sent his son off first, and then his wife, and of how, because of the weather, he took his chances, waited. I tell her what happened when he finally soared himself—how every paper, every proof, every knuckle of everything he'd carried with him—in his pockets, in his suitcase, around his neck—jiggled loose during his flight and fell to the ground in the East. "It was like confetti," I say, my voice getting loud, my sentences like victory punches. "It was like confetti, raining with the rain. And nobody saw it, can you picture that? The guards didn't look up because of the rain. They didn't look up because of *weather*. Because they were afraid of getting a little wet." I put my fist up like Holzapfel himself just rode in. Like he just landed here beside me on his homemade flying fox.

"Crazy," Arabelle says, slow and suddenly wary. "That's some crazy, crazy story, Ada." She's stopped her filling. She's watching me. Those eyes above her bandit face. Those glasses on her forehead, splattered.

"Not so crazy," I say, defensive.

"One in a million chance," she says, "of not getting caught doing something like that."

"Happened before, could happen again."

Arabelle pulls the bandanas off of her face—the first and then the second—and drops them to her neck like coiled-cloth jewelry. She rubs at the pink that freckles her skin, the little bits of blue from my can. "You're scheming, aren't you?" she says finally. "With that boy of yours."

"I'm just talking about flying," I say.

"You're talking crazy, is what you're talking."

"Finish the fill, all right?" I say. "Fill has got to be perfect."

She yanks her bandanas back up, hooks them over her nose. She rattles the can. She molds her pressing finger. She does all of this while watching me, then carries on with the fill.

Left to right.

Third over thirds.

Release at the end of each stroke.

Everything, I think, in its time.

*

When we're done we're done: Our arms are shaking; the cans are empty; the agitator balls are spitting nonsense. I pack my bag, cut the lights, kiss Arabelle's cheek. "Not bad," I tell her, "for an amateur."

"Not bad for a spy," she says, and she laughs, and when she laughs the air turns to crystal, and in the crystal there is pink, but just a little. No one has passed this way all night. The guards have not been bothered. Only now and then have we heard the Alsatian dog in the no-man's-zone bark at a phantom or a shadow, at one of those mine-defying bunnies. We filled and we confetti'ed. We flying-foxed Mr. Heinz Holzapfel, got him to freedom—fat caps and skinnies.

"Home?" Arabelle asks, headed for the bike.

"Not yet."

She gives me a but-I'm-tired-and-it's-so-cold look. I shrug, because it's not like I asked her to come, and it's not like I've not been accommodating.

"You're here, right?"

"So?"

"And I didn't go off looking for Savas. As promised."

"I guess not."

"My reward is your reward. I want to show you something."

We leave the bike where it is, propped up against the wall. I reach for her hand, her furry pink glove, which is pinker now in places and blue in some spots and crunchy, a little worn through on the index finger. We walk side by side, hand in hand, down the narrow alley between Kreuzberg and the Grenzwall 75, the meter of walking space that the East left to us made even narrower by piles of snow.

When we reach the observation post I put my arm across Arabelle's shoulder and guide her up the steep flight of planked steps until we're standing at the guardrail looking out over the wall's sewer-pipe cap. Past the anti-vehicle ditch, the hedgehogs, the control strips, the light poles, the patrol roads, the watchtower, the trip flares, the dog run, the signal alarms, the signal fence, the barbed wire on the other side. Past the bright glare toward East Berlin, Friedrichshain, where the old buildings are fortified and the new buildings are concrete boxes, one room on top of another, every room exactly the same size, one light still on, the rest of it darkness after so much glaring brightness.

"You think they see us?" Arabelle asks, shivering a little. "The guards, I mean."

My eyes track back toward the guards in their yellow-lit room, the steam in their windows, their radio antennae spiking up top. They've got portholes for firing through. They've got a 360-degree view. They've got shoot-to-kill orders if anybody flees, but right now, our graffing done, we are not their enemies. We are safe where we are against this splintery rail, safe watching that side from this side, looking for Stefan. He's out there, somewhere, in the dark. Isn't he?

Stefan. Please. Answer me.

"Do you think . . . ?" Arabelle asks again, but I pull my left arm tighter around her and lift my right hand, marking that one solitary distant light in Friedrichshain with my spray-can finger. It twinkles on and off, yellow and blue. It looks like a star that has fallen.

"That's him," I say, a whisper now.

"Stefan?"

I nod, proud and hurting, but not actually sure, my whole body suddenly electrified with how much I miss him. "He's gorgeous, isn't he?" The light goes on and off, bright and chilled, like one of the glitter sparks in Arabelle's bike seat.

"Yeah," she says. "I guess he is." Squinting as she says it, smiling like she sees, because she's my best friend and because what I have said is true: Stefan is the most beautiful boy in my world. No one can replace him.

"I'm going to need your help," I tell Arabelle now.

"Help how?" she asks, her voice hushed.

"With Stefan and also with Savas," I say.

She takes a step back. She stares at me. I see the questions bulge her eyebrows.

"I didn't know the two were related," she says.

"Of course they are."

"How?"

"Two people trapped in two wrong places," I say, and I'm about to say more, but I stop. Arabelle will understand when I tell her someday. She's my best friend for a reason.

"You're going to have to tell your mother," Arabelle says after a while.

"I will."

"When?"

"When I know what I'm actually doing," I say, and suddenly my teeth start to chatter and there's a clench up in my chest and my knees throb and Arabelle is here, her arms around me.

"Hey," she says. "Hey. You've been sick, you know."

"That isn't it," I say, striking a tear from one eye.

"That's maybe partly it," she says. "Come on." She helps me down the stairs and down the alley. She balances me back onto the bike, takes the seat up front, leans in, and steers. She pedals, steady, all the way home. There are no lights on at the day care. No tiny bootprints in the snow. No letter waiting when I get home. Just the bear on the couch, and the darkness.

FRIEDRICHSHAIN

★

They never gave you your grandfather's body. You never had proof that he died. Even after they knocked his empty coffin into the frozen ground your grandmother went to the Vopos begging—for the bones of him, for the truth—and every time she came home empty-handed. A welt appeared beneath one of her eyes, like an underground tunnel for the tears that lived inside.

She'd waited four years to put his coffin in the ground. She waited another two before she dragged an old chest into the middle of the biggest room and asked for your help. He'd left six shirts and three pairs of trousers; you folded them into their smallest versions. He had a watch that worked and a watch that didn't; you wrapped them both into his flannel scarf, the good one wound and ticking. "Take it," she said. "Pack it," and she meant everything—the stiffened shaving brush, the caked cream, the towel that he'd worn around his waist when he was waiting for the shower to lose its steam, the pom-pom hat, the belt with the torn third notch, the black socks with the gold toes, the windup metal monkey with the rusted metal drums that he'd kept on the counter beside the canister of flour for no reason you could remember, the pair of cufflinks, pretty as stars. You were eleven. You were a thief. You stole from his overcoat pockets and his picture frames. You stole the laces from his boots and the leather patch from the elbow of his sweater. You stole his books and his fishhooks, his homemade bow and his arrows, the map of stars that you pasted up to the ceiling above your head. *Take it. Pack it.*

"Just a few parts and some string," Ada said. "Just a wheel and a harness." She was explaining again how the Great Escapee had taken the pieces of one life to build another life. She was talking about courage. She was saying, The longer you wait, the harder it is, and sometimes you can't know until you decide. She was Professor Ada Piekarz, talking her thoughts over yours, there and not here, basil sprouts and zurna songs in place of interminable brown. "You don't want to be a plumber," she said. "You love me," she said. "Choose."

She wrote her letter in purple glitter glue.

Her one single word: *Now.*

"Open it," Grossmutter had said. Except the seal had already been broken. Maybe it was the Stasi who had read it before me. Maybe it was Grossmutter. Anything could crush a dream. You can't make promises unless you're sure you can keep them.

SO36

*

I sleep inside my own fumes, my hands ironed thin beneath my pillow, my skin too thin for the bones of my hip, which jut into the cushion on this couch like broken sticks. *Now*, I'd written, and I remember last winter when we crossed and Stefan was there wearing a big bear coat and an old man's hat and you could see, even so, his rare boy beauty. He was beside his grandmother, on their side of the wall, and he hadn't seen me yet in my Köpi sweaters, blowing on my hands. It was threatening to snow, or hail. The skies were a thick woolly gray. Cumulonimbus on our side. Praecipitatio on his. The border guards were taking their time. Every now and then Stefan would bend toward his grandmother and offer her his hairy coat. She would shake her head, insist no, and then he would offer again, draping his bear arm around her shoulders, until she finally laughed. *He loves her*, I thought, and I felt terrified, because who belongs to whom? Isn't that what we fear most? Being loved less? Being left out? Being chosen against?

"Hurry, Omi. Please," I said. But we were caged in that line and Stefan was out there with his own life, keeping his small family warm. I was a fool that day when we finally made it through. Wouldn't let go of his hand, wouldn't leave his side, hardly looked at his grandmother, as if what she'd taken was mine. I made Stefan take me out to the balcony and show me the stars.

"It's cloudy," he said.

"I don't care."

I was wearing the bear coat by then. He was wearing an old sweater. His hands were slightly blue. His teeth were chattering. "What's gotten into you?" he said.

"Nothing."

"Ada."

"It's just . . ."

"What?"

"It's that I hate how much I love you, Stefan. I hate this." I pointed behind us to his little room. "I hate that." I pointed to the wall.

"It'll work out," he said, taking me into his arms.

"Not if you don't leave, it won't."

Now, I'd written. *Now. Now.* And nothing's come of it.

FRIEDRICHSHAIN

★

You head west toward the wall and to the idea of her, close. You tilt your head back, exhale your cold-breath cloud, and watch it fold, furl, cut the dark. If she's there, on the other side, she'll know it's you, your hopes rising. *Ada.* You have your old gloves on, a roll in your pocket. You have an extra pair of socks in your bag, a hunk of cheese and bratwurst, the two pompoms you untied from your grandfather's cap; he wouldn't have minded, you're sure of that. The bow you've slung across your shoulder seesaws back and forth whenever the wind picks up, slicing your jacket threads and creaking. Beside it, the cardboard quiver scratches your neck. In the streets the snow is dirtying beneath the tires of the Trabbis. From windows up above icicles snap. It's early, not yet dawn. The dark hasn't died but a pale day will come. The lights are on at the Delikat, in the windows of the early risers, in the weak eyes of the Trabbis, but still: You feel all alone and this isn't a promise. This is you, testing the possible.

By the time you reach the small park on the edge of things, the morning light is coming in. Through a break in the hedge you make your way, snow in your boots, loose snow in your hair. You pace it out. You set your pom-pom target in the nook of the biggest linden tree and measure back. You draw a line with the toe of your boot, slip the bow from your shoulder, your cardboard quiver, and try to remember what your grandfather taught you years and years ago. You were only small. You were only watching. You didn't know he was going away for good. You didn't know that someday you'd be here, in the loneliest big park, on winter's coldest day, trying your luck at shooting arrows straight and free.

Ready now, you remove your gloves. You fit the bow into your left hand and you stand, easy as you can in the mocking brown cold, nocking the arrow into the string. You give the string elbow room as you pull back, all the way back, your right index finger at the line of your jaw and the string near the tip of your nose. When the string is taut, you release, and the string goes snap. The arrow flies off in a wooden wobble—whining away like a misfired missile and waking a bird you hadn't seen in the tree. The arrow sinks at an angle. It strikes at the snow. The unpierced pom-poms sag in the cradle of the tree.

It was just a first shot, you think. A warm-up. Now, your hands cold, you notch the second arrow in, plant your feet, and put more bend into your knees. You pull, release, and follow through. The arrow flies east of your target, lands on the thick of the hedge.

"Nice shot," a voice says, and you turn. It's a tall kid, a punker, his arms crossed and his back slouched up against a smaller linden on the opposite side of the park. He stands there looking disappointed, like you owe him something, like he bought a ticket to see.

"What do you want?" you ask, getting the third arrow into the string and turning your back on the kid.

"You need some help with that?" he asks.

"Not really."

"You sure?" You can hear the smirk in his voice.

"Yeah. Sure." You lower the arrow, look up at the trees that circle the park, as if help is there, somewhere. You turn back and stare at the kid who has stubbornly settled in, one big sneaker up on the base of the tree. He wears a long coat that's way too big, a cheap pair of jeans, and canvas sneakers. He has a black thatch of hair, and you don't know the face behind it.

"Didn't know it was regulation, shooting in a park like this," he says, like he's looking for some kind of conversation.

"Doing no harm."

"The way you shoot, you could."

"What do you want?"

"Name's Lukas," he says, pushing away from the tree now and coming toward you with one hand out—long hand, skinny fingers. The snow fills up the loose places in his sneakers. His coat whips around below his knees. You hear the Trabbis out there, in the street. You hear a bus warming its engine.

Through the snow, into the snow, the kid tromps, but you're not shaking his hand, because he's not invited here. You work the string on the bow and the third arrow instead, but your hands are cold and shaking. If you plant and nock and then release, this arrow's going nowhere.

"You're leaning," the kid says now. "That's your problem."

"Yeah?"

"It's basic," he says.

"You some kind of expert?"

"Sort of."

"I guess it's my lucky day, then."

"Look," he says. "It's easy."

His eyes are black all the way through. There's red in his cheeks where the skin is frozen. He's got a gold ring through the right flare of his nose, a string of leather at his neck, a freckled shell pulled through it. He doesn't look the bow-and-arrow kind, but when he reaches for the bow, you let him take it.

"Some simple rules," he says, very deliberate, something like hunger in his eyes or respect for the mechanics of bow-strings and arrows. "Pull straight back but keep your arms a little bent. Put both hands up to your nose. Keep your shoulders calm and low. It's not your arm that does the pulling. It's the muscles of your back, your shoulder blades."

He shoves his hair away from his eyes and sets himself up for a shot. Lays the arrow across the arrow rest and settles it into the bowstring. He draws back across a perfect straight line, rubs at his jaw with his index finger. Finally he lets the arrow fly. It soars toward the tree, into the pom-pom.

"Aim small, miss small," he says.

You shrug like you don't believe it, like it doesn't matter anyhow.

"You want to try?"

He chooses a fourth arrow from the quiver and hands it to you, like he's being generous with your own grandfather's stuff. You leave him standing there and head for the tree, where the pom-pom is a red heart bleeding. Now one by one you collect your things—the target, the arrow that made the mark, the two of them that didn't, the cardboard quiver.

"What?" he asks.

"I'm late," you say.

"All it takes," he says, "is practice."

SO36

*

I wake to quiet talk and a broken square of sun, the rattle of the gassy pipes that snake through the walls and beneath the floors of this old building, delivering nothing but noise. Beneath their lids my eyes feel hot with the propellant and the fumes. When I breathe I smell the sweet, harsh smell of paint. It hurts on the right side of my head and at the back of my throat, but if I move I will forfeit my advantage.

It comes to me in pieces—the first voice Mutti's, the second not Omi nor Arabelle, not even German. It's the voice of a man who doesn't know this language well, a *man*, and my mother is laughing, that soft *whisk whisk* she does when she thinks no one who's sleeping can hear her. She is telling him to wait. He is telling her no, look, the sky is up. Not the sky. He means the sun. The sun is up, it's time to go; he says it right now, with a twist.

I blink and see fumes. I turn on the couch, sly, not enough to pop the soft kernels inside the old velour pillow. His hair is the color of strawberries smashed and preserved, set aside in a jar. His skin is winter. The bones in his cheeks strut up high and hungry, but his eyes sit crooked on their shelves—the left eye a little smaller than the right eye, and neither eye looking at Mutti.

The morning sun is a mirage.

There's another lover in the kitchen.

So this is the one, I think. The canal one, the heartbreaker. This is the one, and he's back, and my mother is tender, my mother is wearing that long sea-foam dress she wears when she thinks love is near, when she dares to believe in it; she's always falling, my mother. Cut wide at the neck, the dress falls haphazard, exposing the bones of her shoulders—so delicate, so hollow. She holds the Garfield mug by its chipped handle and lets it swing back and forth from the crook of her finger. There's a box of pastries on the table, its string snipped. There's a trail of powdered sugar—two trails. The smoke I smell is from cigarettes, and not from Omi's candle.

"Stay," my mother says again, and the man says no so gently that it sounds like yes. He's standing and she's reaching for his hand. He says something about me, the girl on the couch. She says it doesn't matter.

"I matter," I say, interrupting my silence.

They turn at once, my mother acting like she's so surprised to see me, like she didn't realize until just now that we're squatters and I sleep on an old found couch. It's not their privacy that's been taken; it's mine. It's not her smile that hurts so much; it's her hope.

"Sweetheart," she says, standing.

"What?"

"This is Sebastien."

"No shit."

She glares.

"What?" Her face is flushed, her skin looks wrong in that Valentine dress. She seems surprised (again) that I'm not happy, that I don't remember all the other men and all the other loves and all the despair that comes after.

"Your manners."

"Manners, Mutti?"

"Say hello."

"Hello, Sebastien." Between tight lips, I say it.

I sit upright, pull my knees to my chin. I'm wearing my green sweatshirt with the hood, my yellow flannel pants. I'm wearing a blanket around my shoulders, cape style. Some of my hair has fallen over my eyes. When I squeeze my eyes shut I see pink.

"I have a question," I say, mildly now, a brand-new tactic.

My mother looks hopeful. Please don't look hopeful. "Ask it," she says.

"Does Sebastien love you?"

"Ada!" My name like the snap of a whip.

"I was just wondering," I say.

"Your mother's lovely," Sebastien says. "But of course we only just met."

"What does *of course* mean?"

"Excuse me?"

"In that sentence. *But of course we only just met.*"

Sebastien takes a minute, smiles. He gets his face rearranged, and his posture, too, like dealing with sleep-deprived, pink-haired, brokenhearted almost-sixteen-year-old squatter kids is his specialty. "I'm from France," he says.

"I can tell," I say, "by your German."

"I hear you paint."

"I graff," I say. "Write. With spray paint."

"Maybe you'll show me your work."

"Maybe. If I finish it. If I want to."

"No pressure," Sebastien says, and it's the right thing to say, and I am stumped so I shrug and suddenly I'm not at all interested in the conversation. Suddenly I know—or I remember—that Sebastien will come and Sebastien will go, like all of Mutti's men, and that this is not something I can protect Mutti from, because I've failed every time in the past. Being nice hasn't worked and being mean doesn't either, and there are other priorities, as a matter of fact. There are other people in the world who need much more than Mutti does. I have to find out what Meryem knows. I have to find Savas. I have to make sure that Arabelle will be fine. I have to get Omi her bratwurst. I have to get up, take a shower. I have to mail another letter.

"Sebastien," I say, knocking the hair from my eyes. "It's very nice to meet you." Emphasizing the *very* so he knows I don't actually mean it, and giving my mother a faux smile.

I stand up from the couch, shake sleep fuzz from my foot, rearrange the slack blanket-cape on my shoulders. "You don't mind if I use the bathroom?" I ask, fake-demure.

Sebastien looks from me to my mom and laughs, so ridiculously handsome. "She's just like you promised," he says to Mutti.

My mother isn't laughing.

*

Arabelle's bike was gone, so I walked, my damp hair drying stiff as a board in the winter air. When I turned and looked back, I found my mother in the window, watching, nobody beside her and her eyes too round, and I hated me for the things I'd said. I hated the fact of this fact: I cannot protect Mutti without also hurting Mutti. Or. I have forgotten how that's done.

In the bell tower of St. Thomas Church the nine o'clock chimes ring, crystal pure, and I wonder if Stefan is listening. I wonder if the machines of the Eisfabrik stop to let the chimes through, and if they don't, does Stefan hear them anyway, the way that once, he said, he heard me crying. It was back when I was fourteen and still in school, before my job at the day care. It was the afternoon, the bell had rung, and I was walking the narrow strip between the wall and SO36 when I felt a hard, hot knock on the back of my neck. Spinning, angry, I saw twin-looking brothers with identical hooked noses and slits instead of eyes, slacking Os for mouths. The O mouths were laughing as if they'd gotten me good, as if there was nothing they thought I could ever do—just one of me and two of them between the wall and the edge of the Kiez.

"What for?" I'd demanded. One hand on my hip, one hand on the back of my neck, rubbing hard.

"Because of the freak in you," they'd said. Together, as if they'd rehearsed it.

The chip of steaming coal was at my feet. The heat of its burn was in my skin. In their steamed-up tower beyond the wall, the border guards were watching. Anything could happen in the West, and the guards would let it go. Anything between two boys and a girl, and they'd sit with their feet up and their rifles greased and turn it into a show. I knew that. There were stories. I should have turned and run, shouldn't have still been there when the dare went down. Five marks to kiss me, one of the ugly boys said. Seven marks for tongue.

I was wearing a pair of shoes with wooden heels, a backpack with everything in it. My hair was orange, long, and wild. They were on me like wolves with their filthy snouts, and I fought with everything I had, but they won. The boys won. Left me on the ground with my jacket broke and my backpack split, and I've never walked that part of the Kiez again, and I never told Mutti, but she knew. I wobbled up those stairs and into the flat and she knew, tears in her eyes like she had seen it from her window, like this was history, repeating itself. "Take a shower, love," she said, and I stayed in the heat until it burned me all over, until I was erased by the steam, and even today there's a mark where the hot coal struck and shadows where the welts had risen when I let the water burn, but right then, that day, I couldn't leave the shower, I couldn't turn the water off, because if I did, they'd hear me crying. I was angry at everyone, not just at the boys. I was angry at the guards who watched, angry at Mutti who knew, angry at Omi for the way she watched me, angry at Stefan for not being in the West where he belongs.

If Stefan lived here, it wouldn't have happened.

If Stefan lived here, I would always be safe.

Safe and nobody's freak. Not ever. Safe, and somebody's girlfriend.

Two weeks later, it was our time to visit and Stefan was there, waiting at the crossing as Omi and I exchanged our marks and showed our papers and were finally let through to his side. His wide arms were around me in a second. His words were in my ear.

"I've been so worried, Ada."

I said nothing.

"I thought I heard you crying."

Don't make me start, I thought. Don't make me.

He ran his fingers through my hair. They stopped at the rough patch of the welt where the chip of coal had struck. He stepped back, looked into me, and kissed me on the bad place. Omi was calling, impatient. Stefan wouldn't hear her, wouldn't stop.

"What is this?" he asked.

"It's nothing," I sniffed.

"Don't lie to me," he said. "All right? We promised not to be liars."

But I couldn't say, and I couldn't stop the tears, and suddenly my fists were pounding against his icemaker's chest, my tears were stains on his thin blue jacket.

"It's going to be fine," he finally said. "Whatever it is."

"It will never be fine, Stefan. Okay?"

There wasn't time to explain, and I couldn't.

Stefan crouched down and took Omi's little white suitcase of long-ago photos into one hand. He kept his other hand on me. We all went forward into the smudged air of the East, none of us talking, Stefan as close as he could be. To his flat and through the door and then he put down that suitcase, and we left the grandmothers together, making tea. Out on the balcony, it was just the two of us, and I was mixed up between love and anger.

"You dyed your hair," he finally said.

"Pink," I mumbled.

"You cut it," he said, "like Cleopatra."

And we stood there staring, out over the wall, past the asshole guards, toward the church, down the canal, to the place where the boys had been mean. We stood there and we didn't say a thing. And for a long, long time, that was enough for me.

"It was only a kiss," I finally said. "And it wasn't my choice. Believe me."

*

There's nothing but slush on the ground. The boot prints and shoe prints and cart trails and tires are all obliterations. At the Bethaniendamm the artists smoke outside on the steps, they drink their coffees, they stand huddled together, three to a shawl, but not Sebastien, so far as I can see, with his Frenchified German, his one eye smaller than the other, his first wrong impressions of me. It's early, too early, and I circle the church, walk around to the back that used to be the front, before the wall went up so close. My graffs are how I left them. My blues are radiant, true. Arabelle's fill isn't bad after all. My wall tells a story; it speaks. A boy on a bike sails by behind me, a basket of bread tied to his fender. Two old ladies pass, their chins dipped down, the hems of their aprons dragging beneath the thready edges of their dark wool coats. A skanky dog with mud on its snout takes a big sniff of my ankles, and still I stand here looking at the wall. Bread and Toilet. Tightrope. Boot in the face. I think about Savas and

Meryem, about the things they know, have seen. I think about fear, how it sticks. I think, *If Stefan doesn't answer soon . . .*

If he actually doesn't.

The bells above my head are silent.

The guards in their smeary tower are likely asleep.

A rat with an abominable tail scuttles by.

My graffing is good. My graffing is a promise.

Stefan.

I back away and head off in the other direction, round the red drum of the church. There's much inside—Herr Palinski and his ten-fingered Bach. I walk the distance and lean against the door; it gives. The inside of St. Thomas Church is tall and white and hollow. It feels cratered out by the moon—arched and swollen, ruffling up. Everyone who has ever sung for Herr Palinski has quit, infuriated by his impossible perfectionism. But when he plays his Bach in his black turtleneck all is forgiven, and people say that it's like Bach himself has been resurrected inside the church that God protected from the bombs.

Herr Palinski playing is an artist working and I sit alone with this song that slides against itself and rises high inside the echoing caverns. Any movement I make is a mistake, and so I sit with my feet still and my fingers quiet as the Bach goes out in waves and skims the fluted columns, the walls, the tinted light of the arched windows, the dried flowers from weeks ago. The old part of the song crests against the new part, doubling it, restoring it, and it is not until the song is over that I realize that

I'm not alone in here with Herr Palinski and his Bach. In the far balcony, the reverend sits, his hands pushed together in prayer. He wears his everyday clothes and his California glasses. He lifts one hand and waves, a sign that I should wait, and now I hear his footsteps on the interior stairs. His footsteps, then nothing, then the reverend again, hurrying down the center aisle on his way to me.

"Ada Piekarz," he says.

"Reverend Schindler."

"To what do we owe the pleasure?"

"The Bach," I say, and he nods.

He sits beside me, presses his fingers to his chin, and waits for the next concerto to begin. "No. 5 in F Minor," he says. "The second movement." It's the wedding song, the processional, and it's so goddamned beautiful holy.

"Oh, God," I say, and there's crying in the word. Reverend Schindler slides his big pale hand over mine and nods and that's it, because that's all there has to be when Herr Palinski plays Concerto No. 5. We don't move until the song is over. We don't move until Herr Palinski stands and hurries through his sheets of music, his head bowed, his eyes avoiding ours. The door flies open, the cold air blows through. The door bangs shut again. The reverend takes his hand from mine.

"I have heard about Savas," he says. "And I am sorry."

FRIEDRICHSHAIN

★

There are things that you'll need. There are lies that you'll tell. That night, in your room, you sketch a thousand different versions of a flying fox. That morning you read gravity and physics. You go through the trunk of your grandfather's things looking for gadgets or signs. You scope low on the balcony, pursuing breaks in the walls, narrow channels, passable distances, chances. You go back into your room and close the door and practice your posture with arrows.

When you arrive at the park, he's there, sitting in a crook, a pyramid of dirty snowballs on the ground beneath him, snug against the base of the tree. His feet dangle in their too-big sneaks. He's got a cup of something steaming in one hand.

"You're a little late," he says.

Is it a jab? Is it friendly? You don't know; how could you know?

He shrugs. Swings his legs, loose and long, knocking the dirty hem of his trench coat and exhaling hard, cold, white breaths. He looks like he's been here all night, guarding the linden, angling for practice, getting bored and blaming you. You stare at him through the dawn, across the park. You watch him take a long sip from his steaming cup, blow on the naked flesh of his hands, leave the trench coat open to the black T-shirt, the dangle of chains at his neck. He slurps and jumps and the snow splats, and now he's pulling something out of the ripped lining of his ruined trench coat, all of it hard to see, given the light. He turns back toward the tree, lifts his arms, and curses. He steps aside, and that's when you see what he's done. A puny bull's-eye target, handpainted. Hung by a string from a low branch, but not the lowest.

"What's that?" you ask.

"You can't shoot at pom-poms," he says. "Seriously, man. You just can't." He finds more in his cup. He swallows it down.

There's no waiting this guy out. He's there, and you're here, and if you turn back now, walk away, he wins and you lose all the time you gained by coming long before they'll start looking for you at the Eisfabrik. You ease the quiver to the ground and select an arrow. You unhook the bow from your shoulder, plant your scruffy boots in the slush, nock in.

Click.

"Hook your fingers," he calls to you. "Ease off the grip."

You think he shouldn't stand too close to the target. You think that if he's smart, if he gets you at all, wants to help himself, even, he'll back off, but now he leans forward, his free hand on his bony kneecap, like he's waiting for your best pitch. Like he's doing you a favor.

"It's all in your back," he tells you now. "And in your teeth."

You lower the arrow, the bow, break the stance. You stare at the skinny kid with his black thatch hair and at the birds that have come in behind him—all of them brown, all of them shivery, taking a dirty-snow bath on the far hedge.

"Consistency is in the teeth," he says, straightening now, putting his hands on his hips. "Trust me on this."

"Okay."

"I've got medals," he says. "At home, I do."

He lowers his mug to the ground, rubs his hands together, and goes off on a tangent you can't actually follow about frogs and elastic and the principles of physics. Your hand hooks. Your teeth close. You concentrate all your power in the ridge between your shoulder blades. When the arrow flies, it zings, busting a hole straight through the paint-and-cardboard target before it arcs to the ground and sticks, a headless flower. Out of nowhere, the rabbit returns, twitchy and unhappy, leaving a track of panic in the old snow. Beyond the park and the trees there is the sound of kids singing an old schoolyard song. You remember the song. You're not a kid anymore. But Lukas—the kid—is whistling.

"See that?" he says.

You nod.

"Just checking," he says.

He fits his big hand inside his torn coat and digs out target number two, which is white and blue, painted on old newsprint with a stiff and reckless brush. It comes out crumpled and bent. He snaps it straight, waves it in front of your eyes, makes sure you're watching. He thinks you can be dazzled. He waits.

"What else you have in there?" you ask.

"Where?"

"Your pocket? That coat?"

"Oh, that," he says, his brow crinkling to help him think. "A bar of chocolate, I guess. A pack of pencils. Keys to the bike lock. An old map. My uncle's compass." He seems genuinely interested in the answer to this question. Pleased that you would ask. He tips his chin and salutes, Young Pioneers style. Carries target number two over to the far hedge, where the birds had been busy, but now they fly off, distressed. He prepares a ridge and sets the target upright. He stands there, snow in his shoes, trench coat open, black T-shirt stretched across his boy ribs, pointing at the target—a smaller mark, a bigger distance. You raise the bow. You nock. You're not doing this for him.

"Follow it through," he calls out. "All right? Relax your wrists. Keep your thumb beneath the line of your jaw." He's farther away, so it's harder to hear. It's easier to listen. You know the arrow is through the second you release it. You don't move, don't even blink, until you hear the paper shred.

"And there we have it," he says, throwing his arms up, victory style. He hurdles the hedge, and a Trabbi honks. He returns, the arrow high in one hand, his trench coat flapping as he hurdles back into the park. He plucks the other arrow from the ground on his way toward you. Scoops up his coffee cup. Smiles crooked. Only one side of his face, you realize, actually smiles.

"What's your story, anyway?" you ask, as he slips your arrows back inside the quiver.

"A little of this," he says. "A little of that."

"You planning to show up every day, or something?"

"Aren't you?"

Like you're really going to answer that.

Like you won't look for him again, the next day and the day after that, Lukas with his arrow smarts. Lukas with his targets—handpainted, freshly made.

SC36

*

"MissAdaMissAdaMissAda."

"Yes, honey."

"MissAda."

"She just asks for you," Henni says. "She won't tell me
a thing."

Henni in her bunchy sweater dress. Meryem in the aqua
coat with the loose wool weave. I'd heard the crying from down
the hall and run. I'd opened the door and found them, one
beside the other at the narrow, speckled table, Meryem's fists
to her eyes, Henni's big arm dragged across Meryem's delicate
shoulders, nobody else around and a pot of oatmeal overcook-
ing on the stove, a tea bag gone cold in a cracked mug.

"What's happened?" I'd snapped the burner heat off and
come. I'd stood here, looking from one to the other, trying to
figure it out.

"Don't know. She was dropped off and she hasn't stopped
crying."

"Well, what did her father say?"

"It wasn't her father. Not her mother, either."

"Who?"

"A woman."

"A woman?"

"In a maroon burqa, blue sandals, a stack of bangles up her wrist. That's what I saw, Ada. That's it. She'd had Meryem by the hand. It was early still, so the door was locked. I'd heard her knocking and when she saw me coming, she left. I'd called to her. She didn't stop. She was in some massive hurry."

"And Meryem isn't saying?"

"You see how it is." Henni lets the zigzags crowd into her brow. The floppy charcoal cowl of her dress has swallowed half her chin. She totters on the tiny chair, doesn't take her arm from Meryem, or her eyes from me.

"Meryem, sweetie, I'm here," I say, fitting my too-big butt into the half scoop of the chair on her left side. I try to take her hand, but she needs both fists to hide her eyes. I scan her head, her jacket, her yellow plastic boots, looking for trauma signs, scars, but whatever has hurt her is inside and she's sobbing too hard to try to tell me.

"How early?" I ask Henni.

"Fifteen minutes ago."

"What did the woman say?"

"Nothing. I told you."

For half a second, Meryem swipes her fists from her eyes, then swipes them back, like erasers on a chalkboard. In that split half second I see enough to know she's terrified. There's a crust of something, I see now, on the tips of her boots. Not old snow. Not mud, exactly.

"Meryem," I ask, "can you tell me what's wrong?"

She shakes her head side to side, her long black hair slapping. She kicks her dangling feet. The chair tips. I catch it.

"Would juice help?"

Her hair slaps.

"Will cookies?"

No. She shakes her head.

"I think she needs some privacy," Henni says. "Before the others come." The blush on one side of her face is gone, rubbed off. The blue lines beneath her eyes have smeared. Henni's been watching kids her whole life long. If she knows anything, it's when to be worried. Henni's worried.

I check the flag-faced clock on the wall, the time told in our national colors. Ten minutes before school begins. Five minutes before the others come wheeling and squealing, shouting *Mine*, digging for playdough, bothering Henni for an early cup of something, ignoring Markus and his songs. If Meryem's here like this when the kids come in, they'll all be crying by 10:15; sadness in day care is contagious. I crouch close and fit my arms beneath the weave of her coat, the little pair of elastic-waistband jeans. She kicks and twists, but lets me take her. She knots her arms around my neck and cries harder.

"We're just going to take a little walk," I say.

"Miss Ada." She clings to me like a suction cup and warms my neck with her breath.

*

Markus is heading down the hall when he sees us and stops, asks me with his eyebrows what's wrong.

"Just a little upset," I say, and now he turns and follows me to the door, heaves it open to the wind. Beyond, on the outside walk, I see the twins running ahead of their mother, racing each other to the entrance on this side of the administrative wing. They see me headed in the wrong direction and yank up short. Markus waves them in with insistent hands and the promise of hot chocolate.

"Go on with Markus," I tell the twins. "Everything's fine." I walk fast, my coat flapping behind me, Meryem shifting in my arms. Her black hair gusts with the wind.

"Herr Palinski is practicing," I tell Meryem as we reach the sanctuary door. "Do you want to listen?"

The jug of her chin goes up and down.

"We'll be his audience," I say. "He'd really like that."

"Okay." She shudders. I hurry us deep into the belly of the church, away from the wind that tumbles in behind, toward Herr Palinski, who is still playing Bach like a four-armed man, like Berlin—both sides—is listening. Slowly Meryem eases in, lets me sit with her in a lonesome pew. She tilts her head and looks up, as if the music is coming from high in the church's hollows, or from the tenacious stain of the windows. Her ducky-yellow boots flop sideways. Her back scoops my ribs.

She takes a long quivering breath. She sucks a fingertip. She curls in close and I hold her, remembering Stefan and the next time I visited, six months after the attack. This time it was June. He had borrowed a motorbike from a friend, and a pair of banged-up helmets. We waited until after Omi and Grossmutter had put on their tea and settled. We took the steps to the lobby, then went out, silently, to the street, and climbed on the machine. I was wearing a purple peasant skirt and lime-green flip-flops, the brown T-shirt with the sleeves I'd replaced with the lace of a dress I'd grown out of. I sat on the hem of my skirt, front and back, so that it double parachuted up around me. I let the wind skim through my diaphanous sleeves and pressed against the thin white jacket that he wore, faux leather.

His hair was longer then, toward his shoulders. We buzzed through the streets, weaving in and out of traffic, breathing sideways through our noses. We stayed close to the wall, skirted the checkpoint, traveled south and west, past bars spilling out onto the street, past ladies in winter coats and sunglasses, beneath lines of clothes hung in the brown air to dry, beside dogs leashed to the stop sign posts, past houses divided, the chainsaw architecture of his Berlin. He was taking us to Treptower, to his side of the River Spree, and I said nothing because there was no hearing anything over the spit of the motorbike.

Over the bridge we went and toward the forest. Through the forest and along the splitting waterways, the hairy grasses, the old, clobbered trees, until, through the fence I could see the endless around of the Ferris wheel and the noses of the floating swans of Plänterwald, the amusement park where the Bloc kids go. Stefan cut the engine on the bike and stopped. He lifted the helmet from his head, turned, unsnapped the strap at my chin. He kissed me like he does. On the thin bridge of my nose first. And after that, on the fat part of my lips.

"It's your birthday," he said.

"May is my birthday."

"You were over there," he says. "I was over here. So today is the day."

"If you want," I said. "Okay." He'd gotten taller than before. His eyes were more blue. Sometimes I looked at him and knew what he would be when he was old, but that day, when I looked at him, I remembered how he was as a kid. His head too big for his body. His incisor teeth too short for the rest of his smile.

Outside the entrance gate somebody had filled a low plastic pool with soapy water and had attached loops of thick yarn to sticks. A crowd had formed—kids and parents, grand-parents; it didn't matter. They were all standing there with these loopy sticks, moving them around like a conductor until a breeze blew and bubbles threaded through. Long bubbles, the size of sewer pipes. Funny-shaped things like luminescent trombones. Big soap animals with hovering wings. Cloud alphabets. Wet Slinkys. Only one of the kids in the crowd couldn't be convinced. She was little, stood apart, a pair of leopard-trimmed sunglasses on, a braid attached to her head with a polka-dot bow. She watched the upward drift from an angle, plugged her ears every time one would pop. She was only four or five, but she already knew too much. Or that's what it seemed like to me.

We were wearing the helmets by their straps around our wrists. We fit our hands together anyhow, and the helmets knocked as we walked through the gate and into the park. Stefan said it was my day. He said we could do whatever I wanted to do, but all I wanted was to be with him, to hold his hand, to let the helmets clack. It was more like a zoo than an amusement park—the bright cages and the Quik Cup ride, the little train on the tracks, the wood-necked swans down in the bumper-car pit. All the screams from things that moved too fast. It was making me dizzy and my stomach hurt and we walked the park's edges and across the footbridges until finally I said, "I choose the Fer-ris wheel," and Stefan said, "I knew that you would."

When it was our turn we climbed in, let the guy close the metal door behind us. The little girl with the leopard shades was in the car ahead, knuckling the bar with both fists. When every-one was in and the wheel wound high, I waited, and everything stopped. We could see all of Berlin from there. The churches on both sides. The schools on both sides. The old buildings and the new buildings and the bombed-out places and the barbs and metal and meshes and bricks of everything that divides us.

I leaned toward Stefan. I told him the truth. "Those boys. They hurt me worse than I said."

We were up there in the brown clouds of East Berlin. He looked at me for a long time, his eyes changing color, the muscles in his neck hardening into cords. It was like he couldn't speak, like all the words he knew had been snatched from him.

"Say something," I said. "Why won't you?" Trembling up there. Afraid not just of what had happened, but of what he would think because he knew.

But he couldn't talk, or he wouldn't, and then when he finally did his sentences came out broken, unfinished. "Sons of bitches," he said. "Sons of . . ." Lifting one fist from the bar, beginning to bang. *Bang. Bang.* Our seat swaying. Our world, already halved, falling harder apart.

"Who the hell . . ." he started again. "What were they . . ." His fist still finishing his sentences, his eyes searching mine, the sky so big and so wet and so unsafe, unholy.

"It shouldn't have happened," he said then.

"I know it," I said.

"It shouldn't have. It wouldn't have. If."

"Bastards," I said.

"Worse than that," he said, and sobbed. The only time in all my life that I ever heard him sob.

It isn't mud on Meryem's boots. It isn't snow. The wrong person brought her to school, and she's still shivering, scared, in my arms. Herr Palinski is playing Concerto No. 7, and suddenly I don't want to understand, but I do.

"Tell me, Meryem."

"I saw her dead," she says. "I saw Savas hiding."

"Where, sweetie? Tell me."

"The canal," she says. And then she loses her words, too. She loses her world. Unsafe. Unholy.

FRIEDRICHSHAIN

★

★ Two wooden rollers, preferably beechwood, cut and lathe turned, fifteen centimeters across, two and a half centimeters thick

★ A pair of wooden handles

★ As much half-centimeter steel cable as you can borrow or steal (ask Alexander, come up with a story)

★ Some steel bolts, sure things (the co-op won't notice, not if you take just one a day, not if you have deep enough pockets)

★ Your grandfather's bow, his quiver of arrows (you've practiced enough, you know you can do this)

★ Two kinds of fishing line (one for guidance, one for real)

★   Some kind of spool for the cable, some kind of padding
so the neighbors won't hear

★   Other things you can't think of right now

★   All the luck in the world

SC36

*

I've found the reverend. Henni's come. Out here in the hall I tell them what I know, while inside the classroom Markus sits with the kids on the storytelling rug and teaches them the words to some song. Meryem huddles on his lap holding a stuffed anteater, the long yarn tube of its nose striped green and blue. She doesn't sing. She rocks.

"What do we know?" the reverend asks. Again.

"That she has seen Savas's mother. That she believes she is dead. That Savas is hiding." I will myself to stand very still. If I don't I will start shaking.

"And you believe what she believes."

"There is blood on her boots, Reverend."

He uses the flat of his thumbnail to smooth the strands of his hair. He tips heel to toe, thinking.

"And this was by the canal. Meryem saw her there?"

"She was running after her dog, she says. He must have gotten loose. Or they were playing. Or—I don't know, actually.

Maybe the dog found the body first and started howling. Maybe that's how it was. But Meryem was there. Early this morning. She got close enough. It's not mud on her boots. I swear it."

Henni keeps pulling at the corners of her mouth with one hand. She's stuffed the fist of the other into her apron pocket. She's gone halfway down the hallway twice, to call the police from the church secretary's phone, but each time she's come back—worried, mumbling. "We don't know enough," she's said. "Since when do our police help the Turkish people?" she's said. "How can we tell the police without dragging Meryem down to the station to be grilled, and heaven knows, the child's been through enough." There are a million reasons not to call, and there are a million reasons that she has to, and the reverend's going to rub off the last of his hair if he doesn't stop thumbing it soon.

"I'm worried about Savas," I say.

"I know you are." Henni says it.

"Well, aren't *you*?"

"I'm worried about all of it, Ada."

"And that stranger," I say. "The one who dropped Meryem off. The one in the burqa, who ran."

"Yes," she agrees, her shoulders sagging. "That, too." She turns and watches the kids through the glass pane of the day care door. She smears her hands over the lines in her brow, anxious and undecided, until finally I tell them the only good plan I can think of, the only way out of standing here, still.

"Arabelle," I say. "From the Köpi."

"Who?" The reverend takes his hand from his head and fits it down on his hips. He looks at me through his thick glasses, the horizontal stripe between one lens and the other like a crack in ice.

"My best friend," I say. He looks at Henni and Henni nods, but the reverend shakes his head no.

"We'll have to bring the authorities in," he says. "We'll have to put our faith with them."

"Do what you need to do," I say. I am running down the hall and into the wind.

*

I find Arabelle on the street outside the Köpi, locking her bike to the lamppost, stroking the blue shine of its banana seat like it's some kind of prize pony. She's muffed a scarf around her neck and her hair is wild, her coat unzipped, as if she suddenly doesn't care who knows or not, who might tell Peter.

"Hey," she says, when she sees me. "What's up?" Her eyes are dark except for the click of light in the center, like the flash caught off of an invisible camera.

"She's dead," I say. "Savas's mother. Meryem said." My words in spurts. Choked off. From St. Thomas to the Köpi, by foot—maybe a kilometer. Run against the wind—a good forever.

The light goes out in Arabelle's eyes. "Are you sure?"

"I can't cry right now. Okay? I can't. You just have to help me." Suddenly I see myself in her eyes—the pale-skinned me with the bright pink hair that's grown black and a little bleachy at the roots. I see myself: Ada Piekarz, the most independent girl in all Kreuzberg, begging for her best friend's help because her boyfriend's locked on the other side and her mother's much too fragile. Because she needs help after all.

"What are we doing, then?"

"We're going to the canal."

"What are we looking for?"

"For Savas. He's still missing."

"But the police—"

"The police have been called. The reverend did that. But we need to find him first, we have to, Arabelle. He'll be too afraid if the police show up. He'll run even farther. If he's still running. If—"

"Don't think like that."

"He's just a kid."

"I know."

"It's been days and it's cold and I—"

"Don't do this. All right? We don't have time." She looks from me to the Köpi and back again. She unlocks her bike from the post and rolls it to me, hesitates. "Wait for me, okay? I'll be right back."

"Where are you going?"

"To tell Felice. She'll call the ladies. She'll get them to the shop to talk."

"There are kilometers of canal," I say.

"I'll be quick, Ada. Just wait for me."

And I stand with the wind in my bones.

FRIEDRICHSHAIN

★

How like a cat she has become, padding the floor on small feet. When you look back over your shoulder, she's there. When you study the wall, it's her shadow. She brings you things. Macaroni and cheese. A pair of gloves from the secondhand shop. A mug of coffee. A new wallet that is an old wallet she found in a dresser drawer. Thank you, you say. Why, you don't ask. She sits and she doesn't talk, finger to her lips, eyes closed, thinking.

As if she knows what happened to your Ada. As if she feels the guilt you've always felt. The guilt of absence. The shame of not being there.

Today the sun is in the sky and the wind blows and you are off the schedule at the Eisfabrik, at home in your room, lying long on your bed, when you feel her behind you and you turn. She's brought her book of photographs, the two pieces of its wooden cover laced together with a cord of leather. She holds it like a platter and stands, determined but also uncertain.

"Here," you say, sitting now on the edge of the bed and making room beside you. The mattress shifts—high, low—like a giant playing seesaw with a mouse.

She's careful with the book, turns its pages slow so that the grainy black-and-whites don't slip from their triangle corners. She starts at the start, drawing her finger through time. See how it was, she is saying, not talking. She was once a girl, wearing her hair in vertical curls. Berlin was once not bombs, not razor fences, not men living in boxes near the sky. There are potted plants on windowsills in the boxes she shows me. There are pianos and people who play them and Christmas trees with icicle limbs, and in a corner of a room sometimes, in a wide-winged chair, a woman sits, a boy on her knee.

"Your mother?" you say.

She nods.

"Your brother?"

"Once," she answers.

She turns the pages, moves time ahead. She grows up, and she's a teen. The curls are gone and her hair falls wavy to her shoulders, and sometimes the boy is with her, growing up, and sometimes a second girl, beside her, waves to the camera from above a cup of tea or from the marching arches of Oberbaum Bridge or from a plaid blanket by the River Spree.

"Ada's Omi," you say.

"Yes." Barely a whisper. Closing her eyes. Leaving time where it is. Shifting the book of pictures to your lap, the heavy wood and the leather spine, the black pages with their photographs, and if you turn too fast, the pictures will slip, the story. The two girls and the brother and the mother and the man who comes in and out of the pictures now with a pair of polished shoes, a uniform. He stares at you from the picture, through time. He blows the smoke of his cigarette toward you.

"Your father," you say.

"Yes."

One more picture, and he's gone. Two more pages and now the pages are blank, and they go on, blank for a long time, until you turn and turn and get to the other side, where Grossmutter and Omi aren't little girls anymore, but women with their hair chopped short, the parts under their cheekbones hollow. There is a baby in Omi's arms. Now there is a baby beside Grossmutter. Now the two of them are out in the sun and the streets are rubble and the girls are growing up, and now there's a man and the white frame that runs around the picture cannot hold him in. The top of his head is sliced off. The jut of his elbow. The length below his belt. The corner of the pom-pom hat he is holding in one hand. You draw in a sharp breath, lean forward. Your ribs dent your heart.

"Shhhh," she says, coming close and touching your hand, because you both know how this story turns out. You know what happens to the man too big for the frame. You can't keep turning, because if you do you'll find yourself. You'll find you and him together. Then.

"I'm sorry," you say, and she shakes her head no.

"You're a lot like him," she says. And leaves you like that.

SO36

*

Arabelle pedals. I hold on from behind, my hands high above the swollen cocoon of her baby, my face whipped by the yarn of her hair. It's a little after ten, and the people with jobs are mostly at their jobs and everyone else is in the coffee shops or out on the street, keeping warm by the light of their cigarettes. We smell the market before we get there, see the pluming smoke, the fabric dust, hear the zurna songs, smell the salt pools of the wet cheese.

Arabelle slows her bike and crosses through, wheels us around strollers, baskets, wire carts, recycled paper sacks, the thick-socked shoppers until finally we're through the crowds and over and down along the Landwehrkanal. A dog could get lost here. A kid could run. Someone could be dead, alone. Savas has to trust me.

"Meryem," I had said. "What do you know?" And she had said that it was just this morning, and she had promised that she would not cross the bridge and that when the dog barked she thought he was crying. She had said there was a fire burning. Squatters' kindle, maybe. Or something else.

And then what, Meryem?

She's dead.

Then what, sweetie?

Savas is scared and he's hiding.

Arabelle screeches back on the brakes, drags her foot on the ground, and stops. I slide off and she unstraddles and wheels the bike forward to the iron fence that separates the banks of the canal from the sandy, slushy path; she locks the bike in. For the first time in what feels like years the sun is in the sky, but still the wind blows cold, and out by a splintered dock an abandoned tug shivers.

We flare out, toward the underpart of trees, the hedges and the broken bits of things, the blue-bottle sculptures, the picnic trash, the smooth-faced houses with eyelid windows that nudge in along the banks—abandoned or taken and rotten. By now the reverend has called the police and back at the Köpi the women are gathering. But here and now, it's up to us, and besides, it's me Savas will come to. It's me who has to find him.

Arabelle fans her hands against her baby as she walks. She scans the water with the camera-click light of her eyes. I run ahead, out, back, trying to think like a murderer. Trying to think like a little boy lost.

"Savas!" A flock of pigeons scatter, a loose grebe. From across the canal, punk crackles on a transistor radio. On the muddy bank of the canal, a pair of old swans squat. There are shadows beneath the bridges, but he isn't there. There's a water tank big as some army machine, and I trace its circumference, bend down to my knees, call: nothing.

"Anything?" I call to Arabelle now.

"Not yet."

My words are white puffs. My fingers are cold. In a clump of grass by the shore of the canal a hightop Converse floats like a dirty duck. Beyond the next bridge the path narrows into bramble and low branches, gray slush. My feet are wet through. There's color high on Arabelle's face.

"Do you think Meryem would have gone this far?" she asks.

"I don't know."

"Did she say anything else?"

"Not really. No. A dog crying. The smoke of some fire."

"Maybe we missed something. Maybe, if we walk back, the same way . . ." Arabelle looks past me, into the thicket up ahead. She lifts her hand over her eyes to block the sun. A sleek-coated black cat walks past on four white paws. We watch it go. It tells us nothing.

"We should go back," she says at last.

"I guess."

"Maybe Felice has news. Maybe Savas is there, with the ladies."

She blows air into her mittened hands, pulls her coat across her belly to save her baby from the wind. Lina, if it's a girl, she's said. Peter, if it's a boy. The first red-headed, dark-skinned baby in the world—that's what she calls it, what she imagines. *You'll be Aunt Ada.* I've pictured a tiny thing with camera-click eyes in a house built of yarn, a thousand Turkish stitches. We walk side by side on the slushy path, beneath the silver gray of the weeping trees, the sun a glare and the canal sullen slow as syrup. "Savas!" I cry, and nobody answers, and Arabelle says that I have to be brave. I think of the story I told about fear, and what a liar I am, because I know what fear is, I know how it finds me.

Savas, please come. I am here.

I hear the sound of wings overhead, one of the big magpies from the top of St. Thomas Church. It slaps like it's chained to the tree. Like it's been leashed and it's a war to get free. I hear the sound, and then I see it—the thing Savas has left behind.

"Arabelle?" But she has already seen it, too, and beside me she is running, holding her belly with her hands, tossing the ropes of her hair out of her face, away from the wind, until we both reach the tree where the magpie was, until she can help me up into the snaking branches, where Markus's patchouli-scented purple shawl clings like a nest.

"He was here," I say, and she shakes her head. Yes, because he was here. No, because now he is not.

"Take it," she says. "For the police." Leaning down now and finding a stick and drawing an X to mark the spot.

✿

There are five. They sit in the dark well of the back room behind the shop. Headscarves. Thick socks. Nervous needles. On the walls behind them, hung, cellophaned, nailed, are the sweaters they've made, signs in Turkish and German, photographs of Sandinistas, words stenciled in green: *the world is not a foreign land—there are no foreigners.* Felice has pushed back her dark hair with her hands. She sits on a bamboo stool, higher than the others, a pad of ecru-colored paper on her lap and a portable tank of kerosene at her feet, a wad of Kleenex in one fist. The three hoops in her one pierced ear make little cymbal sounds as she listens.

She doesn't turn to us. She follows the talk.

Arabelle steps in, breathless, her coat open, her hair wild, as now the lady in the orange scarf and green cotton coat jabs her knitting needle toward the room's one window at something she sees, some piece of evidence or story. She knows what has happened; it is clear. She has, like the other women gathered here, borne witness to the private hell of Savas and his mother. She knows what men will do to disobedient wives. She knows what sons will do for their mothers. I feel my heart, cloggy and dense, and now Arabelle walks to the center of the room, and everything goes still. She takes the shawl from the sack she had strapped across her chest, and explains the canal, the tree, the patchouli. One woman then another begins to cry. Others nod their heads, confirming.

Change the story, I want to say. *Change the ending. Please.*

Arabelle's spine curves. Felice's fingers knot. The talk goes too fast, and now the first woman, the orange and the green, lifts one hand and makes a pistol with her fist—cocks it and fires—and I cannot move in my wet socks and boots, cannot think, only

Don't.

No.

Please.

But it's clear. It is too true. The mother is murdered. The son is missing, still. Lost, perhaps or probably. I feel Arabelle's arms around me. I hear the tinkle bell over the door out front, I turn to find the police, but they aren't there. It's Mutti who has come, and Omi behind her—one tiny and one small, both of them rearranged by the wind.

"Oh, God," Mutti says. "Thank God, Ada, for Henni. She said you'd gone out to the canal in search of the boy, but we couldn't find you."

FRIEDRICHSHAIN

★

You make a list of all that could go wrong. The arrow zings south or north, but not west. The cable snaps. The wheels jump the line. The handles pull you crooked. The rabbits will twitch, the dogs will bark, the guard will wake up from his half-sleep, his finger on the trigger. You will be heard. Seen. Found out. Betrayed. You will change your mind. Your body will not be returned. Your Grossmutter will be taken to the station. Your hole in the ground will curdle, empty, without you. She will not love you. She, your Grossmutter. She, Ada.

Do the drawings again.

Test the math.

Figure out a big-enough plan, figure out who, in the West, can help you.

Grossmutter whisper-walks to your room, leaves things behind. A pencil. Hot chocolate. A photograph that must have slipped from its triangle corners. *That's you. That's him. That's us. Here.* She turns the TV up so loud that the ears won't hear what you're thinking. She stands in the threshold of your room, watching, minuscule. Taking a long tour of you with her black eyes. Studying the sack that you've packed and the bulge inside—the rope and rollers, locks and keys, handles and three kinds of wires. Soon it will be test day for the flying fox. You've bought the wire off the black market from a guy in the crane-repair business. You've smuggled hooks from the Eisfabrik. You've practiced every knot you know on the drapery cords and decided that if anybody asks, you will explain that you are practicing for the circus that's come to town; there are signs all over town, pictures of skinny men on the high trapeze, the fantastic heroics of tumblers, midair.

"Know what you're doing, Stefan."

"I'm just—"

"No," she says. "Don't lie to me." The husk of her lips against your forehead.

And then she is gone, and it is you, alone with your maps, your math, your tests, your half-lies. It is Ada, over there, with her wanting and her hurting and her love brighter than color. It is those bastard wolf boys, prowling in an alley, those bastard wolf boys winning because where were you? What did you do?

Nothing is certain, except that this is: Ada cannot be hurt again.

SO36

*

Sometimes you need color to tell a story, and sometimes the whole thing is there in black and white.

"Be careful," Mutti says.

"I am."

"Don't stay out all night."

She'll listen for my boots on the stairs. She'll wait for me to pass through the courtyard and out the gates, into the April night, beneath the rows of flower boxes, where the seeds are starting to split in their dirt. It's near the hour. The bells will ring. Sebastien will place his chin on her shoulder as he does sometimes, his hair a bright red bloom on the sill of Mutti's bones. They have been quiet at night. They have been quiet in the morning. They have let me be, because they know how mourning is.

I've left Arabelle her bike with the soggy streamers in case Peter wants to take her for a ride, her arms barely long enough now to reach beyond their baby. That's what she calls it now—*theirs, ours*—ever since Peter found out. It was just after we knew for sure that Savas was gone and the news wilded through Kottbusser Tor and some people called us heroes, but we're not. It took Meryem and Felice and the Köpi ladies and Henni and the reverend and Arabelle and me. It took the police, in the end, who fanned out along the canal and went farther past the bridge toward the brambles. It took four days. They were found in a room built of stone, a half-shelter. It had been done with a pistol—Savas's mother murdered and Savas dead of heartbreak or of cold, or of so much hiding, or because he did believe in fear, or because he didn't. They found him with his head on her heart, the thin cotton of her headscarf pulled like a shroud across his shoulders.

There will be, it has been promised, justice. There have been stories in the paper, photographs, Arabelle interviewed on the Gastarbeiter problem. "They are not a problem," she said. "They are part of us." Lifting her hands and letting her coat fall free and explaining the circumstance of people brought to a country to serve, the circumstance of women bartered into marriage, the circumstance of little boys who love and who are buried now beneath humped ground—bathed and clothed.

That's when the camera snapped. That's the picture that Peter saw the next day, front page, local paper, and that's how he knew, and that's why he came, and that is why he will stay, why they are together now, an American rebel and an Everything girl with a bike as spangled and streamered and strange as a Kreuzberg parade.

I didn't want to go to the day care anymore. I didn't want to pretend to be fearless when I'm not or tell stories I don't have or stop Markus from teaching his protest songs, because maybe we all need to sing our protest songs, stand up and be counted, and besides, Meryem is gone. The stranger lady in the maroon burqa has taken her home, to the Anatolian farmlands, where Turkish girls have more choice than they do in Berlin and where maybe she will forget, or at least survive, the pictures in her head, the blood on her boots.

"You'll come back," Henni told me.

"I don't know."

"You're always *welcome* back. You are loved here."

But love is not enough. It is not the Great Escape. Isn't Henni old enough, doesn't she see how it is? Doesn't she remember Ancient History? Love is what you give and love is what you want and love is how you wait, but it doesn't save you. Across the long lawn of the Mariannenplatz I walk, the cans of paint clinking in my backpack, the skinnies and the fats rolling between them, the bandanas stuffed in, a chalky pencil losing its tip. Everything's here in black and white. Everything's lit by moonlight—the big belly of the church, the wing feathers of the magpie, the broad doors to the sanctuary, where Herr Palinski's Bach has floated high and fills the round stone hollows. Depeche Mode on this side. Rabbits and dogs on the other. Stefan, who won't answer yes or no.

Just tell me, I wrote last time. *I need you to be honest.*

But nothing comes in the mail for me, and when I stand on the observation deck by the wall and wave, nothing and no one waves back.

You can start to hate a boy whom you love as much as that.

FRIEDRICHSHAIN

★

You have to know whom to trust. You have to see through the punker kid to his heart. You have to wait until he tells you his story because you can't tell your own story first. Telling first is sabotage.

Winter has thawed. Today's sun will rise early through the bundled clouds. Lukas peels his body away from the biggest linden tree as if he were a giant swatch of bark. He's traded his trench coat for a thin tie that he wears loose around his neck. The two slicks of his black hair are struck apart by a bright white part. You haven't seen him for days but you're not surprised that he's come. Lukas doesn't surprise you anymore. Not what he knows. Neither what he does.

You show him what you've brought. You say it's just a game, a little fun you're having: You want to see how a gadget you've been building runs. You let him hold the parts, watch you assemble, see how it is. The lathed wheels and the various wires. The handle you built at the Eisfabrik when the men were outside, having lunch.

"You need an anchor," he says, understanding.

"You bring your Trabbi?" you ask, meaning that pineapple-colored tin can of a car that he drives from time to time.

He nods.

"Your Trabbi would work," you say. "As an anchor."

"How's that?"

"You park it over there," you say, pointing to a place just past the park, beyond the hedge. "Hook the cable to its fender."

"Huh."

"I take the other end of the cable, hook it to that branch in the tree." You point up toward the high limbs of the tallest linden. You help him imagine the tethered cable running at forty-five degrees from the tree branch to the fender. You put the wheel on the cable. You hang from the handles. You fly. "Easy," you say. "Kid stuff."

"Then what?" He rubs his chin and you see what he's had done to his hand—a spider tattoo over the knuckles of his fist. A black spider, a blue web. Some of the lines still scabbed and healing.

"Then what, what? I take a ride. You take a ride. We see if it works."

"Funny game," he says, still rubbing his chin.

"Think what you want."

"Think it will work?"

"I haven't tried it."

"Christ, Stefan. What were you going to do without my Trabbi?" He smiles, a bigger smile than you've seen before. Two rows of sugar-white teeth, small and square as a child's. He turns in his loose shoes and makes his way across the park through the opening in the hedge, the points of his peach-colored tie tipping up in the breeze. You hear his car a little while later, the reluctant engine turning over, the thin wheels rolling across the loose gravel of the street. You climb the tree while he parks the car by the curb on the right side of the hedge and secure the cable, waiting for him to return. When Lukas shuts the engine down, it shudders like a wet dog on akimbo legs. By the time he hops the hedge and returns to you, you're ready for action.

"It's worth the risk," he says, his eyes squinting into the rising sun. He takes the spool of cable from you and trots back toward the hedge, measuring the decline, linden tree to Trabbi fender. The pink part of the day has come up, a dent in the brown and blue sky. From where you sit hunched you watch the early people walk, the small dog at the street sign pee. Two months, you think. Two months you've been coming to this park with your amateur equipment, and nobody's guessed what you want; nobody's stopped you. Archery practice. Gravity tests. You put your secrets out in the open, and it's the safest that they'll be.

You can hardly see Lukas, on his side of the hedge. You see the cable jiggle as he works to make it taut, feel the struggle of it, wait. Truth is, he's right: You need him, you need his Trabbi. If he hadn't been here, you'd have had to wait—for the next day, and the next day, until he was good and ready. Your luck, in these matters, depends on him. And you haven't told him an actual thing.

"Got it!" he yells at last, his words faint, and at the exact same time the cable snaps into a fine forty-five-degree slant, like there's a big fish suddenly on a fishing line. He stands up, waves. There's grease on his face. He finds the break in the hedge and trots toward the tree.

"You go first," he says.

"No shit," you smile. "What did you think?" He shakes his head and spits. Jogs back toward the street where the rusty Trabbi's parked, following the angle of cable.

"All clear," he says, saluting like a soldier.

The light's good now. The streets are less quiet. The peeing dog has gone, left its puddle, but two old men and a couple of kids have come to see what the ruckus is about. In the street, Lukas talks about the circus. He explains extravagantly, with his big fluttering arms. More people come, but it's not quite a crowd, and the police aren't here yet, so there's time, it's time, to fly your fox from the high branch of the linden to the soft stop of the hedge (you'll jump off there, so you don't hit the street; you won't fall far, should the fox fail; you hope it won't fail). You fit the handles to your palms. You slip your feet free of the tree limbs that have held you all this time, shake the muscles in your legs out of their long crouch.

"Ready?" he calls.

Ready.

"Now?" he asks.

Now.

SO36

*

They buried Savas. They wrapped his body white and tucked it neat as a seed into the shallow grave. In the Muslim cemetery, Arabelle translated. Held one of my hands, while Mutti held the other, and beside Mutti, Felice, and beside Felice, Henni, and then the reverend, and then Omi and Markus, the tallest and the shortest, the survivors, hand in hand. We stood along the redbrick wall, listening, our heads bowed, our thoughts on Savas, the little boy with the huge heart, the boy on the bike in the dark. We watched as they walled the hoary earth back in around him:

> *From the earth did we create you.*
> *And into it shall we return you.*
> *And from it shall we bring you out once again.*

Until the grave had risen like a camel's hump, and it was time.

We need to go, Ada.

I can't.

We need to leave him here, in peace.

I could have stopped this.

I still can't breathe. It is too hard, every day, to find my face in a mirror and not to see the mistakes I made, the outcome. I have dyed my pink hair white, roots to end, let the bangs fall in, over my eyes. *Stefan, you bastard, I need you.*

On a wing of black, on an Eastern Bloc wall, on my piece of Kreuzberg, Savas will rise—bigger than all of Stefan's skies. It has been weeks since I last wrote to Stefan. Twenty-four days. "Yes. No." I wrote. "Yes/No. Tell me." And every single day, no answer has come.

Now you will never meet Savas, I wrote.

I loved you, but not anymore, I won't.

Why won't you answer, Stefan?

This will be my last Great Escape. This will be my thirteenth and final panel, and here, tonight, alone, I black it again, my lamps bearing down behind me, my skin spackling with the violent propulsions of paint. Let it be. Let it stain. Let the sweet smell of aerosol be the smell of Kreuzberg tonight. I will black the black until it's perfect. I will wait, again, until it dries. I will trust my own light and my own arms and my own heart as I paint Savas, his crescent moon and star, in eternal, holy white.

I will paint Savas, and he will rise. Give me that much. Make it mine.

FRIEDRICHSHAIN

★

"It's nothing," you tell Grossmutter, but she sees how it is—the long sleeve of your arm torn up and bruised. The hedge didn't stop you like it was supposed to do, and the rollers didn't work, and you'll need ball bearings to keep the axle spinning right, and you can do this, it can be fixed, but in the meantime, your arm is bleeding and you've ruined Lukas's tie. "I don't need the damned tie," he said, as he wrapped your wounds tight in its cheap nylon, as he drove you back home in his Trabbi, the flying fox tossed to the backseat in its broken and assorted parts, the cable twisted as a snake. He dropped you off at the curb and you leaned back in to collect your stuff, fumbling with one hand, one bad-bleeding arm, and he said, "Don't be stupid. I'll see you soon. Get the arm fixed up in the meantime." He drove off before you could stop him, the Trabbi dragging its muffler down the street.

She daubs your wounds with alcohol, the sting of a thousand bees. She uses a pair of tweezers to remove the pebbles and twigs that scraped in when you fell. It hurts like hell. You look away and let her work, calculating the things gone wrong, the stuff you'll have to fix, if Lukas doesn't drive your fox to the other side of East Berlin, if he comes back, like he promised.

You don't even check the time. You're not at the Eisfabrik, and there will be consequences, explanations owed to Alexander, who has been cutting you slack for weeks now, not asking.

"Have you called in?" Grossmutter asks, reading your mind.

"No."

"Be intelligent," she says, picking up the phone and calling the number that she has committed to memory, just in case. "For what?" you used to ask. For this, you guess. The call rings through. You have had an accident, she tells someone. You're en route to the hospital. Yes, she says. Yes. Yes. Then, No. She hangs up, finally. You thank her.

"Get up," she says.

"What for?"

"I'm not lying for you. Let's go."

"To the hospital?"

"Didn't you just hear me?"

She grabs the boxy purse with the silver snap from the closet floor and the paisley brocade jacket from a hanger. She shuffles out of her slippers and into her square-heeled pumps. Now from a hook near the bathroom sink she grabs a terry-cloth towel and wraps your arm, pinning the two ends together with a safety pin she unlatches with her teeth. "Okay," she says, meaning *stand up*. A single key unbolts all four locks on the door.

"Now," she says.

You aren't going to fight her.

She's a mite of a person. You're your grandfather's size. Out on the street you try to protect her. Through the terry towel your deepest cuts still bleed, and you think of Lukas out there, your stuff tossed into the backseat of his Trabbi. He knows more about you than you know about him: where you live. How you fall. He has your flying invention, your future, your life, and he has vanished beneath the brown sky, between walls.

"Stefan, are you listening?" Grossmutter says. She looks up, the folds of her neck dangling from the point of her chin.

"Yes." You've gone six blocks and there are plenty more to go, and the towel has begun to crust and stick to the matted hairs of your arm. The foot traffic works against you—the factory hands, the bell ringers, the paper shredders, the technocrats, the apprentices aproned for work. Their noise crowds you in, their hurry to somewhere, and suddenly you realize that Grossmutter feels safe here, lost within the noise, invisible, unheard.

"Come here."

"I'm right here."

"Closer."

You lean in.

"I know what you're doing," she says. "All right? I am no fool."

You don't agree. You don't deny.

"Promise me something."

"What, Grossmutter?"

"Be smart. Don't make a long goodbye."

SO36

*

In the day Sebastien goes to Bethaniendamm to work on the mural that will make him famous. ("Putting chickens before eggs," Omi says.) In the afternoons and evenings he's here, turning our squatter flat into a color village. He has decided that what we need most are yellow, pearl, and green—a different color for each of our rooms. He's painted checkerboard squares on the narrow bathroom floor, a wire bridge arch over the place where the mirror will be, when and if we find a mirror. He's bought Timur a painted tin and some seeds, commissioned him to grow my mother flowers. It's early May, and the seeds have sprouts. I pass them going in and going out of the courtyard.

He cooks. Mutti eats. We all sit there chewing, Omi deliberate as ever and dark-eyed somber. Mutti's men don't ever last this long. Mutti's never been this happy. Omi keeps chewing and watching, reads in her pearl room or goes out for an afternoon of vanish and twice in these past two weeks she has been gone all day, but she won't confess to where she's been. I smell the East on her, the brown air, but I know not to ask her. I see her packing things, moving things, setting off for the flea markets with the things she doesn't want in her hands. She comes home with coins in her pockets and no more castoffs in her hands.

"What are you doing, Omi?"

She doesn't say. She watches me. She asks me sometimes about Stefan.

"I don't know," I'll say.

"You don't know *what*?" she'll say. Staring at me through half of her eyes.

"I don't know anything about Stefan," I'll tell her. "I don't know anything about miracles."

"You make room for miracles, Ada," she'll say. "Do you hear me?"

She'll say it and leave. She'll do her business in the shadows of her thinning room. She'll go away and come back. The space around her grows bigger.

"Omi," I will say to her. "Please tell me what you are doing." But she has said all that she will say, and I have neither lied nor told her something.

I leave, too—leave when I can. I find myself places to go and things to do, like making a mobile for Arabelle's baby. I draw all the people the baby will know and string them together with hangers and yarn. Arabelle and Peter and Felice and the ladies and Mutti and Omi, and me, too, Aunt Ada—all of us in black and white, stark and true, our mixed-up Kreuzberg blood. I want the baby to know who the world is made of. From its very first days on this earth.

So I go. I sit. I draw. On the park benches and by the sausage trucks. In the shadows of trees, by the canal. Behind the market and in the sanctuary of the church, where Herr Palinski never asks why I'm not at the day care anymore. I use graffiti tricks in miniature, working from memory and intuition.

And sometimes in the afternoon, when I can't not think of him anymore, when it's sadness I feel and not anger, when I think, *What if it's the Stasi taking my letters away, what if it isn't even Stefan's fault?* I wind down around the belly of the church and past the Thirteen Great Escapes and through the narrow lane between Our Side and Their Wall until I reach the observation tower and climb. The green is coming in on the trees over there. Nobody waves when I do.

FRIEDRICHSHAIN

★

Two weeks, the early hour, and Lukas doesn't come. You go to the park every day before starting time at the Eisfabrik and you wait, your back against the middle linden tree, your feet where you fell. They put ten stitches in your arm and the black threads itched beneath your sleeve, and you have tried to stay calm, to swallow past the sick hot spot high in your throat past your tongue. You didn't know him, after all, did you? You trusted the wrong punker guy, and now he has your stuff and he's guessed your story, and he knows where you live, and it's not like you can go to the police for a stolen flying fox, *come on*, and you swear to whatever God there is that if the Stasi come for Grossmutter, you will kill them. You trusted everything to a skinny guy with a spider on his fist.

And what about Ada? What about Ada, waiting, the letters you didn't answer, *couldn't* answer, because What if? What if you said you would come and it didn't work out? What if something went wrong, and you had promised? What if the people who read the letters you write figured it out and came to get you? Losing Ada is nothing next to disappointing her, and losing Ada is enough.

It's getting late. You have nothing to carry but the stitches beneath your sleeve and the jacket you'll need inside the factory of ice. You study the break in the hedge, the tops of cars in the streets, the few people who pass by and stop to study you, as if they're waiting for the circus to come. The church bells from the other side ring. It's starting hour, and Alexander's there waiting, with his clipboard and his careful eyes. "You fell where?" he asked. "In the flat," you said. His letting you lie, again, being his greatest act of friendship. You will never forget Alexander. You'll owe him big time someday.

There's that black cat again, on its white feet. There are the birds, and the sun sticking to the bottom shelf of the clouds that came in fat last night, blocked your view of Kreuzberg. The scope only sees so far. It's losing part of the color spectrum, and its capacity for pink. You stayed out late on the balcony last night, until it was only you and the TV tower, awake.

People in the street, cars passing. The cat rubbing its nose against the rough cloth of your jeans. The whistle of a policeman blows, more of a screech than a note, and it's time to go. You step away from the tree. You're halfway through the park when you hear the muffler yanking itself down the street.

Lukas?

You turn in the direction of the noise, and you wait. You see the pineapple Trabbi shivering at the curb, shutting its minuscule powers down, spitting Lukas out of its driver's seat. You stand where you are, not moving. You watch him trot, but slow, around the park's perimeter, toward the break in the hedge, across the hard earth, toward you.

"Hey," he says, like it hasn't been two weeks, like you're not just standing there with a look of something fierce on your face.

"What the hell, Lukas?" you say, when you can speak.

"Man," he says, lifting your pack off his back. "There was some work to do." He crouches down by your feet, works the zipper on the pack. Talks down, toward the ground, so you crouch, too, and he unzips, and he talks, and you interrupt him.

"Two *weeks*," you say.

"This was never going to work," he says. "Good thing you went first." He chuckles.

"I thought you were gone," you say.

"I was busy," he says, and by now the flying fox is out of the pack and on the ground, laid out for your inspection, much improved, according to Lukas, who is still explaining how you didn't lathe the grooves deep enough, didn't counterweight the handles, needed a stronger harness strap. *No wonder you fell.* You'll be late to the Eisfabrik if he goes on like this, but he doesn't stop, until finally, abruptly, the words shut off and he stares at you until you shift your gaze and look directly in his eyes.

"Corner of Schmollerstrasse and Bouchestrasse," he says.

You shake your head, shrug, and say that you don't understand, he's talking crazy, and *two weeks, man.* You thought he'd absconded.

"Listen, Stefan. It's perfect. I went there. I looked. The place is abandoned. We'll make like repairmen."

He's done his own math. He estimates a distance of fifty meters from the five-story house in the East to the four-story house in the West. He talks about how lucky we are that the house on our side is taller than the house on the other—how the angle of our escape will give our flying fox just enough speed. Yeah, sure, there's a watchtower in the midst. But if we play it right and wait until late dark, the guard might not see us.

"What are you talking about?" He could be a trap, you think. He could be Stasi ears, testing you. You have to test him back. Study his face, wonder what he knows and whom he's told. Like suddenly, after all these mornings in the park, and everything between you, and everything neither of you carefully said, you have to get the kid's credentials.

"No. 68-A Bouchestrasse," he presses on. "Neukölln. I've got friends who will be waiting for us there with a car."

"Friends?"

"All right, not friends. My brother. One guy, but it's enough. He made the escape last time, and I didn't. I got lockup. Twenty months. He's there, and I'm here, and there's nothing for me, unless I jump. It's our time to jump. I knew you were the one the first time I saw you shooting lousy arrows in the park."

Your heart pounds in your gut, against your throat. You keep your eyes on him, saying everything fast and everything in a whisper. He fiddles with the fox the whole time so that anybody passing will assume he's teaching you new laws of physics and mechanics. "We'll need more cable," he's saying. "We'll need a fishing line."

"You're assuming a whole hell of a lot."

"Listen to me, okay? Just listen. The building at Schmoller-strasse is empty, and the chimney is solid stuff, thick and strong enough to take our weight. The skylights above the attic lead directly to the roof. We'll make them think we're repairmen. Carry our stuff in during broad daylight, and stay up there until any thinking guard is asleep in his watchtower. We fish the three lines out, one after another, over the wall. We hook our wheels in. And then . . ." He lifts his eyebrows like they can swoop off his face. He throws his hands up high, then scatters them, far as his skinny arms can reach. To Neukölln.

He keeps talking. You half hear him. You know this part of the story. It's what you've thought through, drawn up, imagined, tested over and over, every day, while you weren't making your promise to Ada. It's the arrow, shot straight, that will take the fishing line across the gap above the wall, over the watchtower, the dogs, the rabbits, the sharp grass, the blaring lights, the hedgehogs, the guard with his radio on, the death trap. It's Lukas's brother—maybe—who will anchor the line to the fender of his car, and when the tug comes, when the first line is secure, when you get the sign, you'll knot a thicker line to the fishing line so that it too might be pulled across the gap. Now there's only the cable to send on in just the same way— its one end tied to the heavier line and pulled across the gap. It's the cable, one half centimeter thick and steel, that will carry you across the sky. The cable that will run like a rail from the house in the East to the house in the West, at a momentum-gaining angle. You'll belt in, unhook your lathed wheels, take a strong grip of your handles, and take your freedom ride. Ten seconds, no more, no less. You know this. You've dreamed it. You let Lukas talk. You have to.

"What are you talking about?" you ask, when he finishes his story.

"You know exactly what I'm talking about," he says.

"Why do you think . . . ?"

"Are you serious, Stefan? You've been leaving the East since I met you."

You study him hard. He studies you harder. He shows you with his hands, again, how it will all go down, how it can happen. He announces the risks and he wipes them away. "Worst thing of all," he says, "would be not to try." The spider on his knuckle walks as he talks. His hair falls into his eyes. Out in the street the traffic is starting. There's a group of kids on the park's other side, singing the Pioneers' song.

"Since you met me?" you finally ask.

"Since the very first day."

"Why didn't you say anything?"

"Because I didn't have to, man."

"You didn't have to?"

"It's all over your face." You bring your fist to your cheek, like you could rub the look away. You bring your eyes to his, and they are clear, black, honest.

"When?" you ask.

"Two days," he says. "May 22. Meet me there. Bring what you have. I'll bring the rest. You'll need socks for the outsides of your shoes—silence, right? You'll need sandwiches, pop, because you'll be hungry. You're a repairman, remember. Dress like one. And tell no one, right? Not a word."

"There's somebody on that side who needs to know," you say.

"Write me a note. I'll get it to her."

You don't ask how he knows it's a she. Your face isn't built for the Stasi.

SO36

*

I see her coming from a long way off, her bike streaming, her hair wild, her belly cradled by the handlebars. She's wobbly, out of balance, in the channel between two walls. She sees me up on the observation tower. Lifts her hand. Calls, "Hey!"

"Hey." I stand up. My butt's cold. I watch her wiggle down the path, then stop. She wears a Columbia University T-shirt and a pair of boy's shorts. Her legs are dark in her tan, high-heeled boots.

"You should be careful," I say.

"Yeah? And you shouldn't be so hard to find."

"Isn't it Tuesday?"

She nods.

"Shouldn't you be at the Köpi?"

"Uh-huh."

"Then what are you out here for?"

She looks up, scans the clouds—the pink and blue fat candy clouds that came in last week and have stayed. She touches the sapphire ring she wears on a chain at her neck. "From Peter," she said, when I asked her. She pinky fingers the tattoo by her eye.

"Special delivery," she finally says.

"Excuse me?"

She walks the bike to the wall and leaves it there. Climbs the stairs to the deck, where I'm still sitting. Heaves herself up, one railing clench at a time, because that baby is that big. She hands me an envelope—all taped shut, not postmarked. She waits for me to open it. I don't know the handwriting.

"Can't be for me," I say.

"Why not?"

"Don't know that writing."

"It says your name. See? Right there. Open it, Ada."

I turn the thing over. It's torn up and beat. It has my first name, no last name, no stamps.

"Who's Lukas?" Arabelle asks.

"I don't know any Lukas."

"Hmmm. That's funny."

"What's funny?"

"Because this Lukas guy went to a lot of trouble to get this to you. Five different messengers, from what I heard, until it landed with Felice, at the Köpi, and it's a good thing that I was there. He had directions: *Deliver to Ada.* I'm following my orders, thank you."

"You've lost me."

"For Chrissake, Ada. Will you open the thing?"

"I'm getting to it," I say. But I'm trembling. I search for the click-light in Arabelle's eyes, draw in my breath, and hold it.

FRIEDRICHSHAIN

★

You stand beside her on the balcony looking out on Berlin. The parts that belong to you, the parts that belonged to her, once.

"What will you do?" she asks, "when you get there?"

"Love Ada," you say. "Apply to university. Become a Professor of Stars." You don't know if that's enough. It's all you have for now. *Tell no one,* Lukas had said, but he doesn't know Grossmutter. He doesn't know about all the people in her life who have left. About how cruel you feel, leaving her. Choices. Consequences.

She smiles. A tooth just past her incisor is missing, something you hardly see, but now you do, now you try to freeze everything about her, remember it just so, frame the picture. Ada was wrong. Grossmutter loves you. She loves you enough to let you go, to let you think that you can teach her to see, to let you believe that she'll stand on the balcony scoping, that she will actually find you. That you aren't being cruel, but self-preserving. That you are being not just a boy-friend, but a man. She understands. At last and finally you know this.

"The world is here," you tell her, showing her the knobs and things on your grandfather's old scope, the way the focus can be changed, the light. You show her the star maps, and how to read them. You show her the dome of St. Thomas and the birds you can just make out, roosting up there in their nests.

"Look for your mother," she says, listening but not bothering to try it out. Looking at you, not through the scope. "When you get there. She'll want to see you."

"How do you know?"

"Because I'm a mother, Stefan, and I was one before I was your grandmother." She has tears in her eyes, but they aren't angry tears. You try to see all her past faces, her future ones. If you want to see something at night, look past it, you told Ada. You look past your grandmother. You look toward her. You wonder when you'll see her again.

"I found something," you tell her. "In Grandfather's trunk." She steps away from the scope, leans back against the railing, as if it can brace her for whatever is coming. You swallow past the lump in your throat, dig deep into your pocket. You feel around with your hand, present her his gift in the night.

"I think he'd want you to have these," you say. Tears in your eyes now, the whole night and your Grossmutter blurring.

"Oh," she says, laying her hand on her heart. "Oh. His cufflinks." You have had them made into earrings. You screw one onto each ear. She shines like two stars, like love is.

"Someday," she says, "the wall will come down."

And you hug her so hard you feel your own bones pop.

There's nothing easy about it.

SC36

*

"Stop crying, Ada, and tell me." Arabelle is insisting, but I can't. We sit on the tower steps, side by side, my face in my knees, the note in my hands, Stefan's handwriting. Arabelle smooths my peroxide hair with her fingers, tries to lift my chin, but all I can say is the one word, *Yes*, until finally I give her the note to read, because there's no way that I could read it out loud myself.

> *No. 68-A Bouchestrasse*
> *May 22. Midnight More or Less.*
> *Yes.*

"What the hell?" she asks, whispering.
"Tomorrow," I say.
"But," she says.
I shake my head—up, down, sideways. "Somehow," I say. "Somehow."

"Could it mean anything else? Are you certain?"

I pull the paper from her hand, run my splattered nail across the words, look up at the light in her eyes. "*Yes*," it says. "See, *Yes*, Arabelle. Stefan is finally coming."

She stares at me for the longest time. She doesn't ask me questions. Then, with her arms and her baby and her love, she stands. With all of that and more, she lifts me. We are two best friends, on the observation platform, dancing, creaking the wood beneath our weight, creaking the nails inside their joints. We turn at last and face the East, and both of us start waving.

"He's coming," she says.

"He is," I say.

"I'll finally get to meet him."

"Oh, God," I say, "is it actually happening?" and she says, "I guess it is," and all of a sudden, just like that, I feel a wave of big sickness overtake me. I crumple to the step, start crying.

"What?" Arabelle asks, stooping down beside me, holding her belly out of the way. "What's wrong now? What's happened?" She looks all around, east to west, sky to earth, looking for the source of the trouble.

"But what if he doesn't make it?" I say. "What if—?"

"No, no, no," she says. "Not at all. You can't be afraid, Ada. Not now."

"I know," I say. "But—"

"No buts now, Ada."

But all of a sudden there are so many buts. Stefan failing. Stefan being found out. Stefan losing. Me losing Stefan.

"It will be all my fault," I say, a whisper.

"Listen to me, Ada. You listen. What fault is freedom? What fault is love?"

FRIEDRICHSHAIN

★

He's there, in the pineapple Trabbi. You're dressed like the plumber you'll never be. Your grandfather's bow and arrows in brown wrapping, your things in a box, your cable around your neck, your overalls saggy with tools. It's a dead-end neighborhood, pressed up against the wall. It's quiet, but you're even quieter—old socks pulled over your boots, only whispers between you, as you lug your things in now, one thing after the other, behind Lukas with his hair tucked into a cap.

There are five stories in this abandoned place, just like Lukas said. Each story turns wide around the square staircase. When you reach the top, you set your things aside and unroll the blankets where you'll work, and only after you have sound-proofed this place as best as you can does he say, "Look at how perfect it is." He lifts the skylight, an easy path to the roof. He shows you the chimney, how sturdy it is, how thick its brick and mortar are; enough, he says, to hold the cable fast.

He points across the way, to No. 68. You see—don't need his help—the guard in the watchtower. The guard has left his radio on. He's playing an illegal station.

Who is a hero?

What is right?

You make your choices, and after that, you live with them.

You see, you say. You see it all, and it is day, still, and it will be day for hours. You have plenty of work you must do. You have plenty of waiting. Whenever there's noise in the street, or a neighbor talking, you're sure that the Stasi are listening.

"Breathe," Lukas says.

You want to.

It will go on like this. It is like this. Hour after hour. Noon toward dusk. Dusk toward evening. He's brought sandwiches and you've brought pop. You've brought a photograph from your Grossmutter's album, the last gift that she will give you. "The three of us," she said. "Don't you forget." You were young once. You had a grandfather. There were three of you in a burgundy room, and in the picture she is smiling.

When you talk, and you hardly talk, you talk in whispers. The rest of the time you remember. Ada, your pink-haired girl. Grossmutter at the scope. Your mother, still missing. Your grandfather. *Man of the house.* You remember that first morning in the park, your fingers brittle with the cold and the bowstring unruly, and you remember Alexander, just yesterday morning. "See you around, Stefan," he said, gentle, like maybe he knows what you are up to, maybe he wishes he were leaving, too. But how could you know? How could you ask him?

"Four arrows," Lukas says now. "That's all we've got." Four arrows, three kinds of string, a chimney sturdy as the linden tree, two flying foxes with the wheels lathed right, the ball bearings balanced in, the handles well dispositioned for the flight, the harness that will hold us, but what difference can a harness make? If we jump the line, the guards will see us. They shoot to kill in the East. The dogs are down there, waiting. The guy's in his tower, and maybe he's sleeping to some rasping lullaby.

"Ready," Lukas says, half a question, and you say, "Now."

"You go first," Lukas says, unwrapping the arrows. "Aim small," he says. "Miss small. Remember the important stuff."

You hold your breath. You set your teeth. You stretch the blades on your back. *I'm coming*, you think. *I'm coming, Ada.* There will be no turning back.

SO36

*

The last time I saw Stefan I was a pink-haired girl who had never hated her boyfriend because she loved him so much. I'm not who I was. I'm no Professor of Escape. Sebastien's moved in and Omi's moving out. She made one more trip East; I watched her go. She came home, and hugged me hard, and that is how I knew.

Yes/No. What kind of choice is that?

"You can't go," I told her, just this morning, which feels like years ago, centuries, another time.

"You know that I have to."

"But I love you, too," I said, crying. "I wasn't *trying* to choose. I want you, too, Omi. Don't you know that?"

She pinched my chin into her hand. She made me look into her eyes. She told me to listen with great care. "Enough is enough, Ada," she said. "I don't need my freedom. I just need someone who understands. Stefan's grandmother and

I understand each other. We will be happy together. We will be fine."

"But you'll be so far away."

"I'll be right across the wall."

"But I'll have stories to tell you. Bratwurst to share."

"I'll be looking out for you. You know that I will."

I looked at her, wondering, Would I see her again? Would I be allowed to travel, this way and that? Would I be black-listed by guards who will finally know that I am the reason for this? That I am the Professor of Escape. That I forced a decision. That I made others choose, and by their choosing I changed the shape of family. "Your Mutti has what she needs now," Omi said, meaning Sebastien, meaning happiness and love. "And you're going to have what you want. And Katja says that she's learned the way the telescope works. I'll look for you. I'll find you."

She kissed me on the part of my platinum hair, ran a finger beneath each of my eyes. "You're all grown up," she said, "and you're beautiful, Ada. You make sure that boy always remembers that."

"He will."

"You make sure that you remember."

I nod. I cannot speak.

Omi won't be there when I get home. Her pearl-colored room will be empty. Sebastien and Mutti will be sleeping side by side. There's bratwurst in the oven, getting soggy, and it will not be for her.

It's just Arabelle and me in the dark tonight. It's just us because Mutti knows nothing; we haven't told her yet; we can't let her hope and hurt, she's still too fragile, and besides: I am all out of words, I am done with explaining. I pedaled all the way to Neukölln, and Arabelle clung, and here we are, standing by the curb of this beat-up building with a tile roof. There's a man sitting on the lid of his car, watching us.

I look up and down the street, wondering from which direction Stefan will come. I check the skies, hold Arabelle's hand. Her baby is kicking and dancing in there. Her hair is bike-ride wild.

"He was there," she tells me about the guy at the car. "At the Köpi. He was there. I saw him yesterday."

We watch him again, and he's watching us. We choose to trust, because we have to.

"What do you think?" Arabelle asks, after an hour has gone by, and the night has grown chilly, even for May in Berlin. It's a little past two, and the clouds of both sides of this city are high—plattering cirrus and the cumulus. I remember my wall of heroes, my every splatter of paint, my Savas, my Omi, tiny Katja. It's quiet out here. The buildings are dark. The grebes and the magpies are sleeping. The man with the car is still waiting, watching the sky and watching us, his arms crossed, his long black hair tied back with a ribbon.

It's just as the wind starts to blow through that I hear a sound. Just then when the man stands, upright, steps away from his car, looks up.

"Did you hear that?" I ask Arabelle.

"Hear what?" Her hands on her belly, her round eyes bright. Our feet balanced on the curb of the street.

"Up there." I point toward the sound of the zing, the little whistle in the weather, the sudden skitter-clatter against a roof. Arabelle looks up, too, and the man keeps looking, and now he runs toward the sound and stops. Something has hit the roof of the building next door. Something's wrong. The man pulls his hand along the black sheen of his hair and walks back, paces now, keeps looking skyward, looks worried.

The second time something whistles through, it stops again in another wrong place. The man runs and stops. He turns around. He looks straight at me, calls my name.

"Ada Piekarz?" he says.

"Yes?"

"I'm Lukas's brother," he says.

"Okay."

"There are only two arrows left."

"The flying fox?" I ask, and Arabelle tightens her grip around her hand and presses her other to my heart, hard.

"Yes," he says. "But the wind is messy."

I can hardly breathe, or see. I crunch the bones in Arabelle's hand.

"Have faith," she says.

I am suddenly desperate, terribly hot despite the chill in the night. I want to race up the stairs of No. 68 and fling myself out onto its roof and stretch my hands like a trapeze artist and catch the world's most beautiful blue-eyed boy in my arms.

Jump, I would say. *I am here for you, Stefan. I love you, Stefan. I so completely do.*

"Two more chances is a lot of chances," Arabelle is saying.

"But maybe not enough," I say, and my eyes are wet, almost too wet to see how, now, the third arrow has already begun zinging itself straight over No. 68 to us. The third arrow is well on its way. Diving and zagging and dropping into the bushes that press up against this house.

"Help me find it!" Lukas's brother says, and in an instant, Arabelle and I are at his side, digging through the sticks and the dirt with our hands, feeling for the sharp prick of the third arrow with the invisible fishing line tail.

"Goddamn it," Lukas's brother says. Pushing through dead leaves, crunching through bush sticks, coming up muddy and empty. He plunges back in, and now Arabelle's down on her hands and knees, her baby belly in the low grass of No. 68 where, a Turkish miracle, the lights are not on yet. I'm patting down a tall bush, squeezing my hand between every branch, taking the thwack of the green against my face, until suddenly I feel it. I run my fingers along the arrow's blade to find the shaft. I yank it free, and the fishing wire is still attached. I am in possession of arrow number three. I am the lucky one.

"Here!" I say, and the man says, "Hurry," and we help him, best as we can, pull the fishing wire toward us until another thicker wire comes through and next a cable, thick and steely, everything scraping our hands, pulling the paint off my flesh, making the baby inside Arabelle tumble, until the man has all the thick cable he needs, and he secures it to the fender of his BMW 525 with the tools he brought for the job, like he does this every ordinary day. We wait for something, I'm not sure what, and when it happens, the man nods, jumps into his car, and turns the key in the ignition.

"Watch out," he says, driving to make the whole thing taut. He hops back out onto the street now, so that the three of us stand—this man, Arabelle, and me—watching the sky, watching the cable, watching for Stefan and for this mysterious Lukas, watching and waiting for freedom. The wind is blowing hard. The clouds are going crazy. I can't remember cloud names or star names or anything Stefan has taught me. I need him to teach me forever.

"They're anchored in," the man says, because the cable line goes heavy, tauter than it was, and now we stand there listening, the three of us—for the wind, for the clouds, for the stars, for the whir like wings, coming for us. There's a sudden thud on the roof of No. 68—on the east-facing part of the building we can't see. Seconds go by, and there's another thud, and then there's the loud sound of shouting. Deliberate. Defiant. Joyous.

We made it! We made it! We made it!

Voices from the rooftop. Voices no Eastern Bloc guard can do a thing about.

I can barely breathe, can barely stand up. Only fractions of my eyes can see, but I know for sure: He is up there—against the sky, inside it. Stefan has come home. He's come for me.

AUTHOR'S NOTE

In the early hours of March 31, 1983, Michael Becker and Holger Bethke were heard singing and shouting in the attic space of an apartment house in West Berlin. They were twenty-three and twenty-four years old, a plumber and an electrician—two East Germans who had spent many months scheming their way to freedom. They had ziplined there by way of wooden rollers and a quarter-inch steel cable—traveled 165 feet, east to west, seventy feet above the East Berlin death strip, in close proximity to a watchtower guard.

Failure was a real possibility, but it wasn't an option. It could have meant death. It would most certainly have meant imprisonment and deprivation in a part of the world, East Berlin, that had been cordoned off from the West ever since the first barbed wall was thrown down among a surprised citizenry on August 13, 1961. Friends were separated from friends. Lovers from lovers. Employees from their jobs. Parents from children. The world had cracked in two. A socialist state on one side. A federal republic on the other. And so it would remain until November 9, 1989, when the East German government, responding to tremendous civil unrest and international pressure, announced that those who had been living the proscribed lives of East Germans could, at last, travel west. The wall was coming down.

The official estimate of deaths associated with attempted escapes across the nearly hundred-mile "Anti-Fascist Protection Rampart" stands at 136. Many historians suggest that the number was much higher. The official number of successful escapees, or defectors, has been placed at some 5,000.

When I traveled to Berlin in the summer of 2011 I discovered a city palpably alive, brilliant with color. I stood before memorials. I cried inside museums. I touched pieces of the old graffiti wall and imagined the ache of being separated from people I loved, from landscapes I yearned to see. I hung out with artists and talked to jewelers and stood at the Brandenburg Gate past midnight in a wash of rain. I heard the great Berliner Dom swell with the sound of a cappella song, and watched the clouds, and got lost in Kreuzberg and didn't mind for a second. I was interviewed—an impromptu moment—by schoolchildren who wanted to know what I saw in their city and what had drawn me to it. I used my hands in an attempt to explain. Words were not enough.

I did not go to Berlin in search of a novel. I went in search of understanding. It wasn't until several months later that Tamra Tuller, my editor, began a conversation with me that resulted, finally, in this book. Tamra had gone to Berlin, too. She had recognized the city's power. She had wondered what might happen to a story set in Berlin, and she shared that wonder with me. I began to read, furiously. I began to dream.

The brave escape of Michael Becker and Holger Bethke inspired one fraction of this story. So did the memoirs of Eloise Schindler, the wife of Reverend Martin Schindler, who did indeed lead St. Thomas Church in the early 1980s, sanction its day care, manage its notoriously mercurial (and talented) Herr Palinski, form a community with Felice and the Köpi, and make a caring difference among Kreuzberg squatters, foreigners, and artists. The scholarship of many, including that of my friend, Paul Steege, provided answers and insights.

Still, this is a work of fiction. The historical facts of Becker, Bethke, the reverend, Herr Palinski, the day care children, the Turkish immigrants, the political agitators, and Felice were all but starting places. *Going Over* is, in the end, imagination set against the very real backdrop of a stunning era. It's what might have been, and who could have been, inspired by men and women of integrity and courage.

I hope that my selected source list will lead you toward a greater understanding of a city, a people, a time.

Now, most essentially, some words of thanks. First, Tamra Tuller. This book simply would not exist without her. She invited me into a conversation. She shared stories of her own Berlin travels. She asked questions, but she never pressed.

She said things—quietly, as is her way—that strengthened my resolve to find this story's proper center. I loved every minute of working on this book. I loved writing it for Tamra.

Second, Heather Mussari. Heather knows a little something about art, and a little something more about graffiti. She knows about pink hair, girl power, acts of courage, and beauty. Ada gets her light from Heather's soul. It's hard to explain. It just happened.

Third, Annika Duesberg. Annika is German, born and bred. She brought her big heart and impeccable English to my country more than eleven years ago, and we have shared a love of dance and gardens. Annika read a late draft of this book to help safeguard me from errors. She was insightful. She was thorough. She was essential, and I am grateful. Any errors that persist are mine alone.

My agent Amy Rennert is integral to my writing life, and for her care through the years and her enthusiasm for this book, I am grateful. To Ginee Seo, Kim Lauber, Lara Starr, Ann Spradlin, Jennifer Tolo Pierce, Wendy Thorpe, Claire Fletcher, and Johan Almqvist, deepest thanks for believing so deeply in me and in this story. Sincerest thanks to Michael Green and Jessica Shoffel of Philomel for the conversations and blessings.

Great gratitude to my generous father, who helped make our trip to Berlin possible, and who keeps reminding me to live right now. Deepest thanks and love to my husband, Bill, who traveled with me to Berlin, who gave me room to cry, and who agreed to stand out in the rain at midnight, trying to capture that city with a camera's eye. And forever love to our son, Jeremy, who was in London when we were in Berlin, making another city his own. Jeremy's encouragement, intelligence, consistent kindness, and unwavering interest in the work that I do is bedrock. When I don't think that I can see something through, he reminds me that I can.

SELECTED SOURCES

Anonymous. *A Woman in Berlin: Eight Weeks in the Conquered City, A Diary*. Translated by Philip Boehm. New York: Picador, 2005.

Ash, Timothy Garton. *The File: A Personal History*. New York: Vintage, 1998.

Buckley, William F., Jr. *The Fall of the Berlin Wall*. Hoboken, NJ: John Wiley & Sons, 2004.

Funder, Anna. *Stasiland: Stories from Behind the Berlin Wall*. New York: Harper Perennial, 2003.

Gay, Nick. *Berlin Then and Now*. San Diego: Thunder Bay Press, 2005.

Hensel, Jana. *After the Wall: Confessions from an East German Childhood and the Life That Came Next*. Translated by Jefferson Chase. New York: Public Affairs, 2004.

Kúnos, Ignácz, comp. and transl. *Forty-Four Turkish Fairy Tales*. Illustrated by Willy Pogány. London: George G. Harrap & Co., 1913.

Mai, Markus, and Thomas Wiczak, eds. *Writing the Memory of the City*. Årsta: Dokument Press, 2007.

Major, Patrick. *Behind the Berlin Wall: East Germany and the Frontiers of Power*. Oxford: Oxford University Press, 2010.

Martinez, Scape. *Graff: The Art and Technique of Graffiti*. Cincinnati, OH: Impact Books, 2009.

McElvoy, Anne. *The Saddled Cow: East Germany's Life and Legacy*. London: Faber and Faber, 1992.

Rice, Leland. *Up Against It: Photographs of the Berlin Wall*. Albuquerque: University of New Mexico Press, 1991.

Rottman, Gordon L. *The Berlin Wall and the Intra-German Border 1961–89*. Oxford: Osprey Publishing, 2008.

Schindler, Eloise. *West Berlin Journal: Stories of Culture, the Cold War, and the Kreuzberg Kiez*. Lexington, KY: CreateSpace Independent Publishing Platform, 2011.

Schneider, Peter. *The Wall Jumper: A Berlin Story*. Translated by Leigh Hafrey. Chicago: University of Chicago Press, 1983.

Steege, Paul. *Black Market, Cold War: Everyday Life in Berlin, 1946–1949*. New York: Cambridge University Press, 2007.

Taylor, Frederick. *The Berlin Wall: A World Divided, 1961–1989*. New York: Harper Perennial, 2007.

Yurdakul, Gökçe. *From Guest Workers into Muslims: The Transformation of Turkish Immigrant Associations in Germany*. Newcastle upon Tyne: Cambridge Scholars Publishing, 2008.

The following magazine stories, films, and Web resources were critical to my research:

Berlin Wall Memorial
http://www.berliner-mauer-gedenkstaette.de/en/the-memorial-12.html (accessed 04/01/13)

Busting the Berlin Wall: Amazing Escape Stories
http://www.cbc.ca/documentaries/passionateeyeshowcase/2009/berlinwall/interactive.html#/START (accessed 04/01/13)

Chronik Der Mauer
http://www.chronik-der-mauer.de/index.php/de/Start/Detail/id/1453512/page/1 (accessed 04/01/13)

Dornberg, John. "Daring High-Wire Ride to Freedom." Illustrated by Michael Dudash. *Popular Mechanics*, November 1983, 78–81, 119.

Newmuseum: Berlin Wall
http://www.newmuseum.org/berlinwall/riseandfall/trying.htm (accessed 04/01/13)

"Swoops Across Wall: Family Makes Daring Escape," Berlin AP, *The Spokesman-Review*, July 30, 1965, 3.

Rise and Fall of the Berlin Wall: History Channel Documentary, produced by ZDF Enterprises, 2009, A&E Television Networks.

The Story of the Berlin Wall by Thierry Noir http://www.galerie-noir.de/ArchivesEnglish/walleng.html (accessed 04/01/13)

BORDER MARKER

THE BERLIN WALL

ANTI- VEHICLE CRASH BARRIER

CONTROL STRIP

ACCESS ROAD